STAR WARS®

EPISODE IV
A NEW HOPE

VOLUME TWO

BASED ON THE STORY SCREENPLAY BY
GEORGE LUCAS

SCRIPT ADAPTATION
BRUCE JONES

PENCILLER
EDUARDO BARRETO

INKER
AL WILLIAMSON

COLORS
CARY PORTER

LETTERING
STEVE DUTRO

COVER ART
DAVE DORMAN

BACK MATTER ART
ADAM HUGHES AND
MATTHEW HOLLINGSWORTH

DARK HORSE COMICS

Spotlight

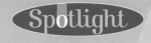

VISIT US AT
www.abdopublishing.com

Reinforced library bound edition published in 2010 by Spotlight, a division of the ABDO Group, 8000 West 78th Street, Edina, Minnesota 55439. Spotlight produces high-quality reinforced library bound editions for schools and libraries. Published by agreement with Dark Horse Comics, Inc., and Lucasfilm Ltd.

Library of Congress Cataloging-in-Publication Data

Jones, Bruce, 1944-
Star wars, episode IV, a new hope / based on the screenplay by George Lucas ; script adaptation Bruce Jones ; penciller Eduardo Barreto ; inkers Al Williamson and Eduardo Barreto ; colors James Sinclair ; lettering Steve Dutro. -- Reinforced library bound ed.
v. <1-4> cm.
"Dark Horse."
ISBN 978-1-59961-621-6 (volume 1) -- ISBN 978-1-59961-622-3 (volume 2) -- ISBN 978-1-59961-623-0 (volume 3) -- ISBN 978-1-59961-624-7 (volume 4)
1. Graphic novel. I. Lucas, George, 1944- II. Sinclair, James. III. Dutro, Steve. IV. Barreto, Eduardo. V. Williamson, Al, 1939- VI. Dark Horse Comics. VII. Star Wars, episode IV, a new hope (Motion picture) VIII. Title. IX. Title: Star wars, episode four, a new hope. X. Title: Star wars, episode 4, a new hope. XI. Title: New hope.
PZ7.7.J658Std 2009
741.5'973--dc22

2009002015

All Spotlight books have reinforced library bindings and are manufactured in the United States of America.

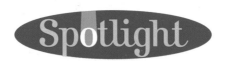

Episode IV

A NEW HOPE

Volume 2

While transporting the Empire's secret plans for the Death Star to Rebel leaders, Princess Leia's ship is apprehended by Darth Vader.

Droids R2-D2 and C-3PO alone escape to the desert planet Tatooine, where R2-D2, carrying the secret plans, reveals to young Luke Skywalker a message from the Princess for Obi-Wan Kenobi.

When R2-D2 leaves to find Obi-Wan, Luke follows. Together, the boy and Obi-Wan—a former Jedi Master—hear Leia's plea for help. With the Empire in pursuit, they quickly hire smuggler Han Solo and his first mate Chewbacca to take them to the Princess.

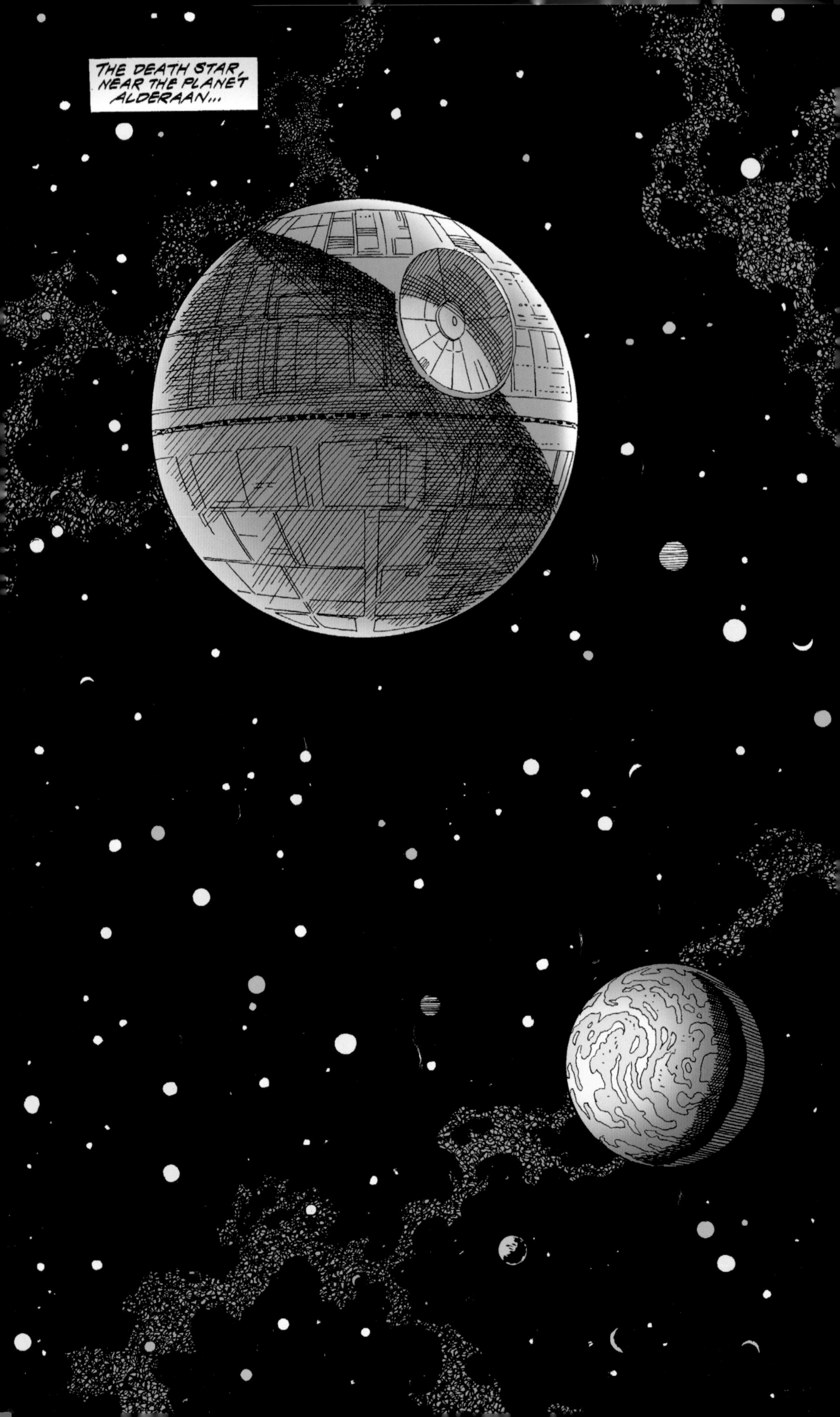
THE DEATH STAR, NEAR THE PLANET ALDERAAN...

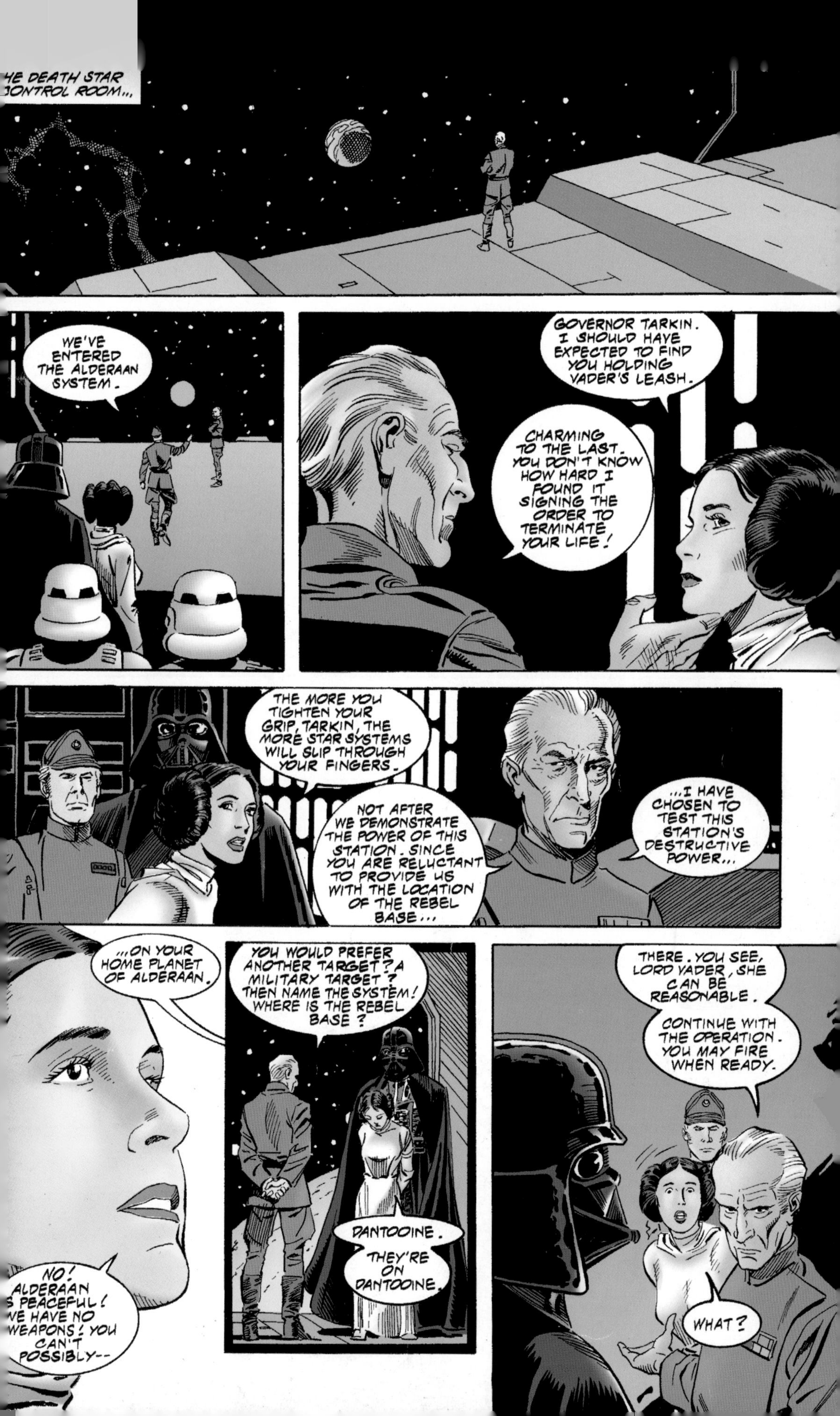
HE DEATH STAR
CONTROL ROOM...
WE'VE ENTERED THE ALDERAAN SYSTEM.
GOVERNOR TARKIN. I SHOULD HAVE EXPECTED TO FIND YOU HOLDING VADER'S LEASH.
CHARMING TO THE LAST. YOU DON'T KNOW HOW HARD I FOUND IT SIGNING THE ORDER TO TERMINATE YOUR LIFE!
THE MORE YOU TIGHTEN YOUR GRIP, TARKIN, THE MORE STAR SYSTEMS WILL SLIP THROUGH YOUR FINGERS.
NOT AFTER WE DEMONSTRATE THE POWER OF THIS STATION. SINCE YOU ARE RELUCTANT TO PROVIDE US WITH THE LOCATION OF THE REBEL BASE...
...I HAVE CHOSEN TO TEST THIS STATION'S DESTRUCTIVE POWER...
...ON YOUR HOME PLANET OF ALDERAAN.
NO! ALDERAAN S PEACEFUL! VE HAVE NO WEAPONS! YOU CAN'T POSSIBLY--
YOU WOULD PREFER ANOTHER TARGET? A MILITARY TARGET? THEN NAME THE SYSTEM! WHERE IS THE REBEL BASE?
DANTOOINE.
THEY'RE ON DANTOOINE.
THERE. YOU SEE, LORD VADER, SHE CAN BE REASONABLE.
CONTINUE WITH THE OPERATION. YOU MAY FIRE WHEN READY.
WHAT?

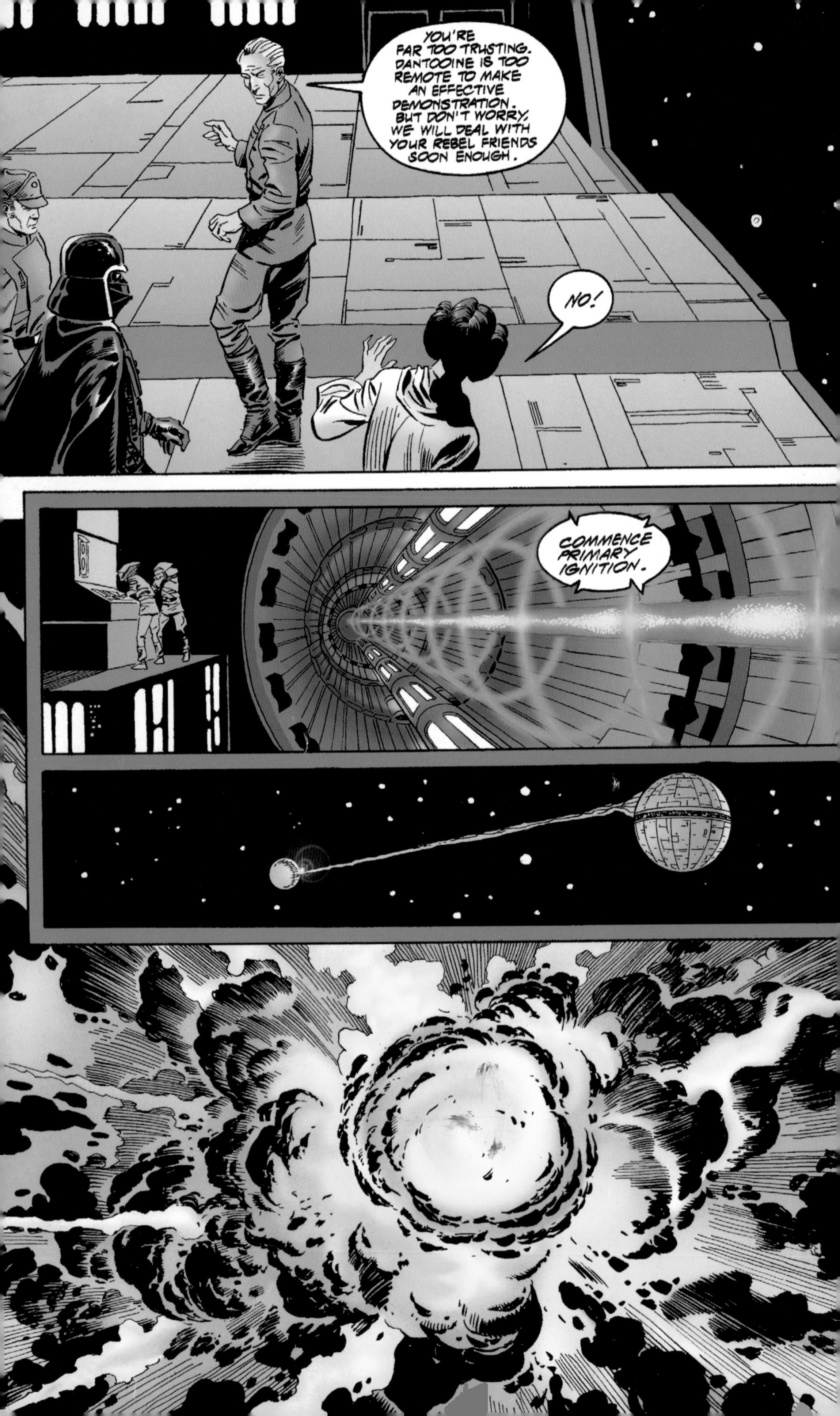
YOU'RE FAR TOO TRUSTING. DANTOOINE IS TOO REMOTE TO MAKE AN EFFECTIVE DEMONSTRATION. BUT DON'T WORRY, WE WILL DEAL WITH YOUR REBEL FRIENDS SOON ENOUGH.
NO!
COMMENCE PRIMARY IGNITION.

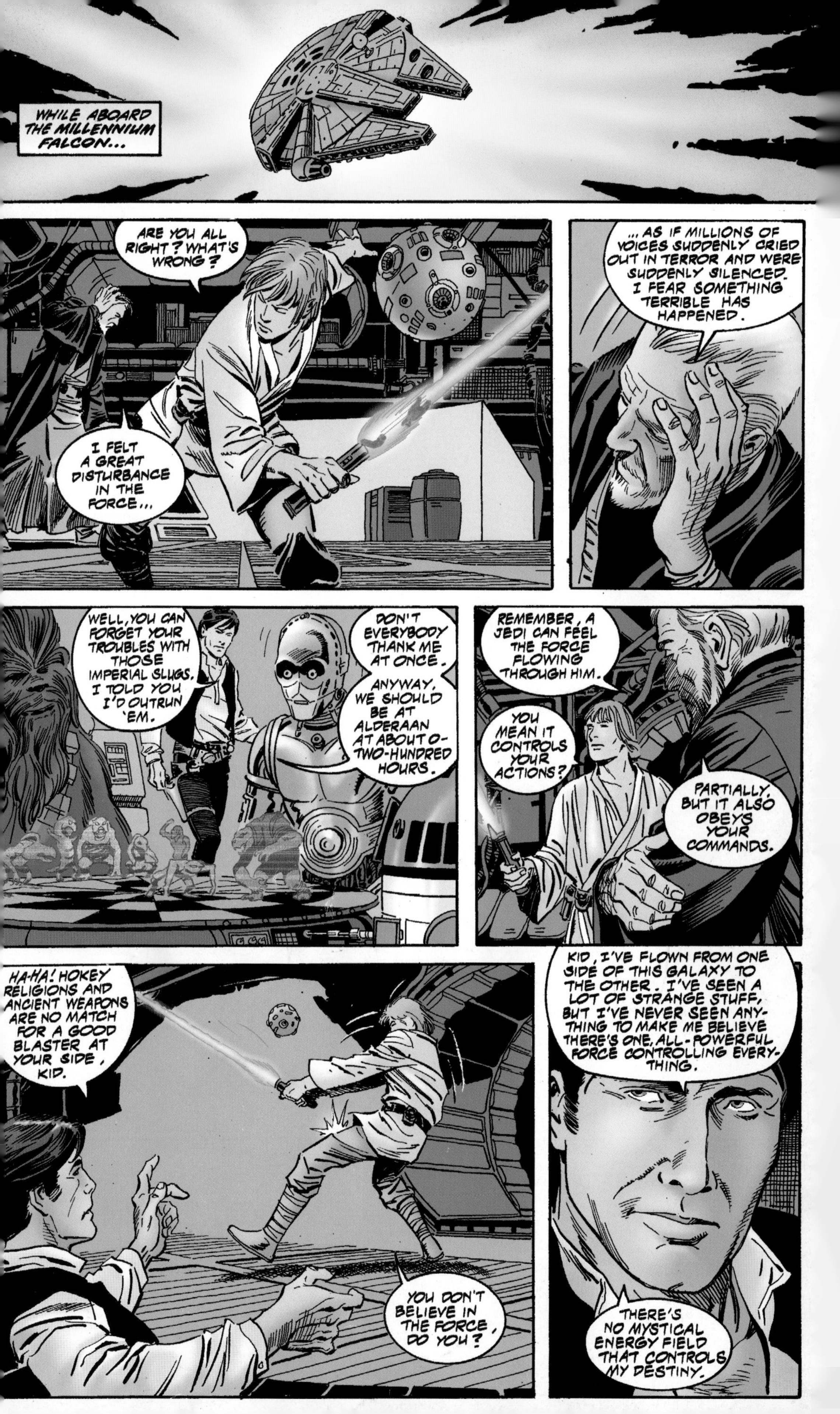
WHILE ABOARD THE MILLENNIUM FALCON...
ARE YOU ALL RIGHT? WHAT'S WRONG?
I FELT A GREAT DISTURBANCE IN THE FORCE...
...AS IF MILLIONS OF VOICES SUDDENLY CRIED OUT IN TERROR AND WERE SUDDENLY SILENCED. I FEAR SOMETHING TERRIBLE HAS HAPPENED.
WELL, YOU CAN FORGET YOUR TROUBLES WITH THOSE IMPERIAL SLUGS. I TOLD YOU I'D OUTRUN 'EM.
DON'T EVERYBODY THANK ME AT ONCE.
ANYWAY, WE SHOULD BE AT ALDERAAN AT ABOUT O-TWO-HUNDRED HOURS.
REMEMBER, A JEDI CAN FEEL THE FORCE FLOWING THROUGH HIM.
YOU MEAN IT CONTROLS YOUR ACTIONS?
PARTIALLY, BUT IT ALSO OBEYS YOUR COMMANDS.
HA-HA! HOKEY RELIGIONS AND ANCIENT WEAPONS ARE NO MATCH FOR A GOOD BLASTER AT YOUR SIDE, KID.
YOU DON'T BELIEVE IN THE FORCE, DO YOU?
KID, I'VE FLOWN FROM ONE SIDE OF THIS GALAXY TO THE OTHER. I'VE SEEN A LOT OF STRANGE STUFF, BUT I'VE NEVER SEEN ANY-THING TO MAKE ME BELIEVE THERE'S ONE, ALL-POWERFUL FORCE CONTROLLING EVERY-THING.
THERE'S NO MYSTICAL ENERGY FIELD THAT CONTROLS MY DESTINY.

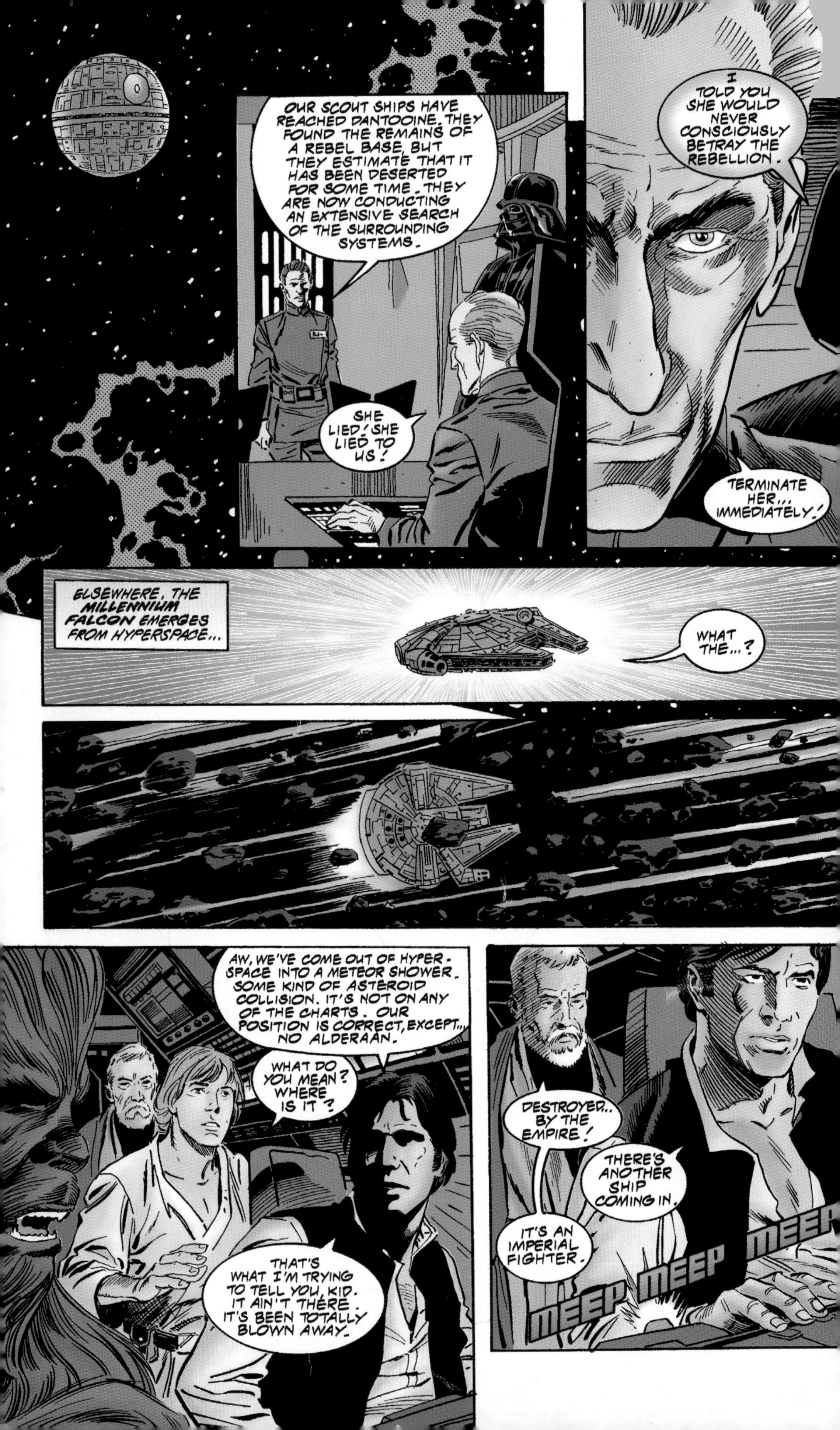

OUR SCOUT SHIPS HAVE REACHED DANTOOINE. THEY FOUND THE REMAINS OF A REBEL BASE, BUT THEY ESTIMATE THAT IT HAS BEEN DESERTED FOR SOME TIME. THEY ARE NOW CONDUCTING AN EXTENSIVE SEARCH OF THE SURROUNDING SYSTEMS.
SHE LIED! SHE LIED TO US!
I TOLD YOU SHE WOULD NEVER CONSCIOUSLY BETRAY THE REBELLION.
TERMINATE HER... IMMEDIATELY!
ELSEWHERE, THE MILLENNIUM FALCON EMERGES FROM HYPERSPACE...
WHAT THE...?
AW, WE'VE COME OUT OF HYPER-SPACE INTO A METEOR SHOWER. SOME KIND OF ASTEROID COLLISION. IT'S NOT ON ANY OF THE CHARTS. OUR POSITION IS CORRECT, EXCEPT... NO ALDERAAN.
WHAT DO YOU MEAN? WHERE IS IT?
THAT'S WHAT I'M TRYING TO TELL YOU, KID. IT AIN'T THERE. IT'S BEEN TOTALLY BLOWN AWAY.
DESTROYED... BY THE EMPIRE!
THERE'S ANOTHER SHIP COMING IN.
IT'S AN IMPERIAL FIGHTER.
MEEP MEEP MEEP

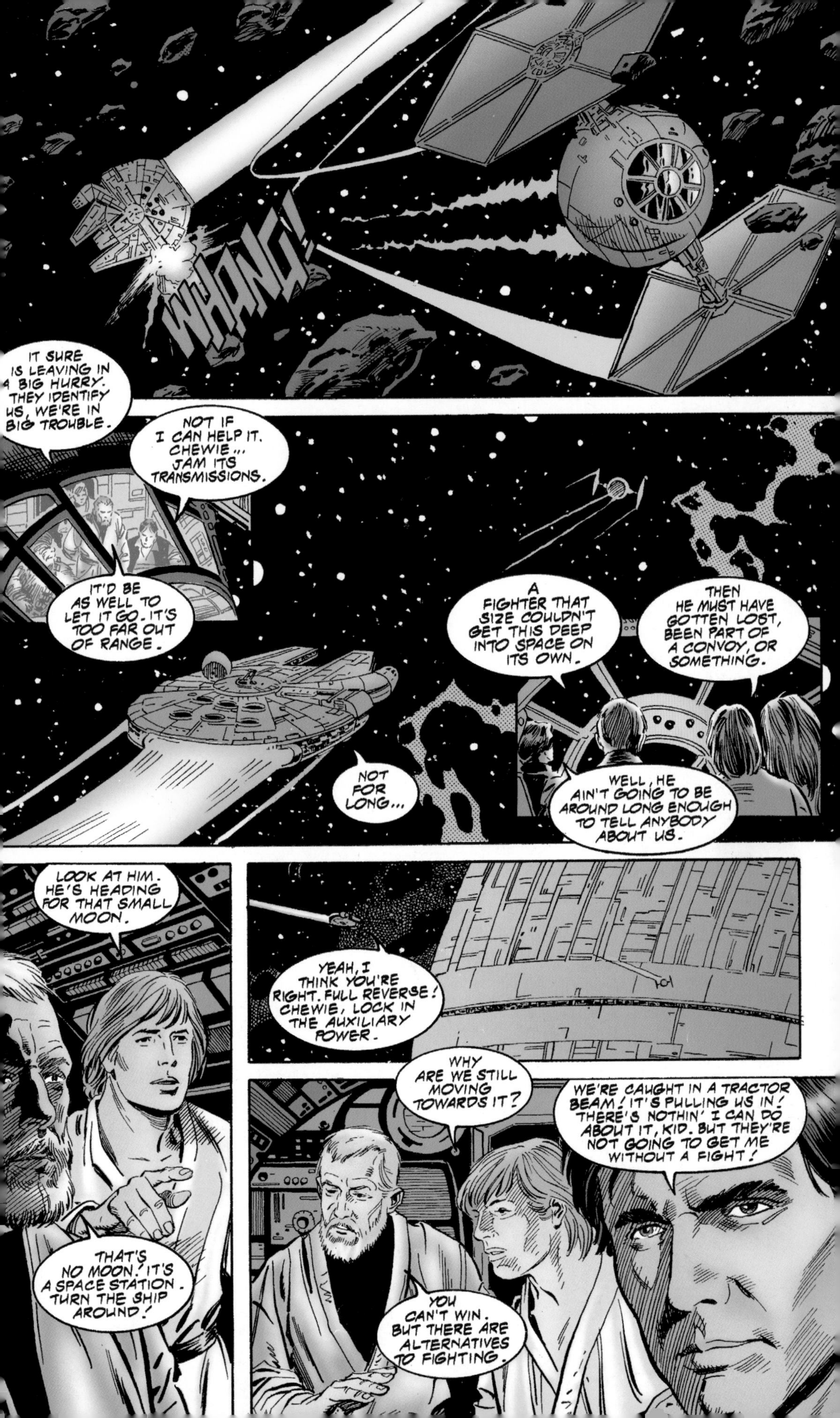
WHANG!
IT SURE IS LEAVING IN A BIG HURRY. THEY IDENTIFY US, WE'RE IN BIG TROUBLE.
NOT IF I CAN HELP IT. CHEWIE... JAM ITS TRANSMISSIONS.
IT'D BE AS WELL TO LET IT GO. IT'S TOO FAR OUT OF RANGE.
A FIGHTER THAT SIZE COULDN'T GET THIS DEEP INTO SPACE ON ITS OWN.
THEN HE MUST HAVE GOTTEN LOST, BEEN PART OF A CONVOY, OR SOMETHING.
NOT FOR LONG...
WELL, HE AIN'T GOING TO BE AROUND LONG ENOUGH TO TELL ANYBODY ABOUT US.
LOOK AT HIM. HE'S HEADING FOR THAT SMALL MOON.
THAT'S NO MOON! IT'S A SPACE STATION. TURN THE SHIP AROUND!
YEAH, I THINK YOU'RE RIGHT. FULL REVERSE! CHEWIE, LOCK IN THE AUXILIARY POWER.
WHY ARE WE STILL MOVING TOWARDS IT?
WE'RE CAUGHT IN A TRACTOR BEAM! IT'S PULLING US IN! THERE'S NOTHIN' I CAN DO ABOUT IT, KID. BUT THEY'RE NOT GOING TO GET ME WITHOUT A FIGHT!
YOU CAN'T WIN. BUT THERE ARE ALTERNATIVES TO FIGHTING.

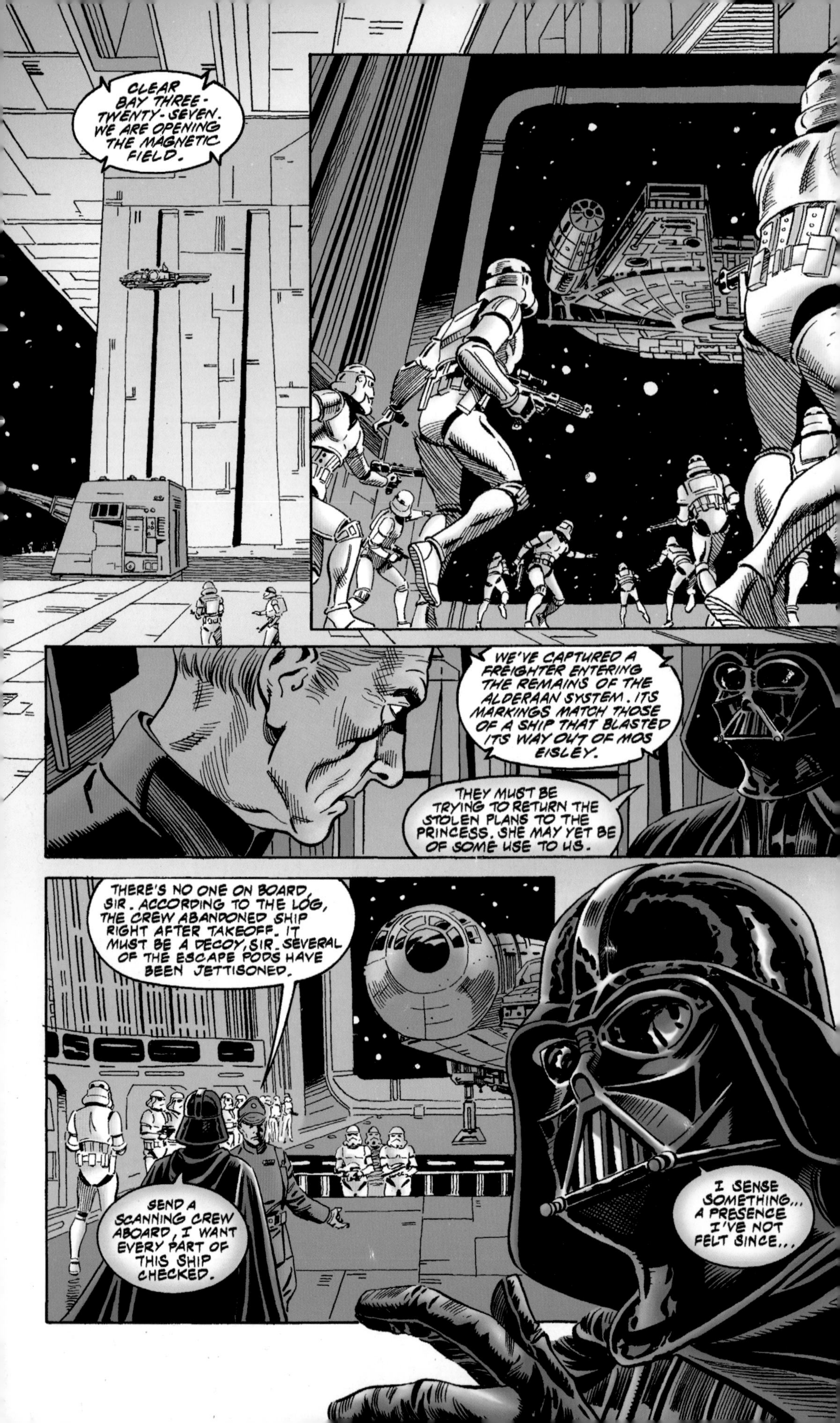
CLEAR BAY THREE-TWENTY-SEVEN. WE ARE OPENING THE MAGNETIC FIELD.
WE'VE CAPTURED A FREIGHTER ENTERING THE REMAINS OF THE ALDERAAN SYSTEM. ITS MARKINGS MATCH THOSE OF A SHIP THAT BLASTED ITS WAY OUT OF MOS EISLEY.
THEY MUST BE TRYING TO RETURN THE STOLEN PLANS TO THE PRINCESS. SHE MAY YET BE OF SOME USE TO US.
THERE'S NO ONE ON BOARD, SIR. ACCORDING TO THE LOG, THE CREW ABANDONED SHIP RIGHT AFTER TAKEOFF. IT MUST BE A DECOY, SIR. SEVERAL OF THE ESCAPE PODS HAVE BEEN JETTISONED.
SEND A SCANNING CREW ABOARD, I WANT EVERY PART OF THIS SHIP CHECKED.
I SENSE SOMETHING... A PRESENCE I'VE NOT FELT SINCE...

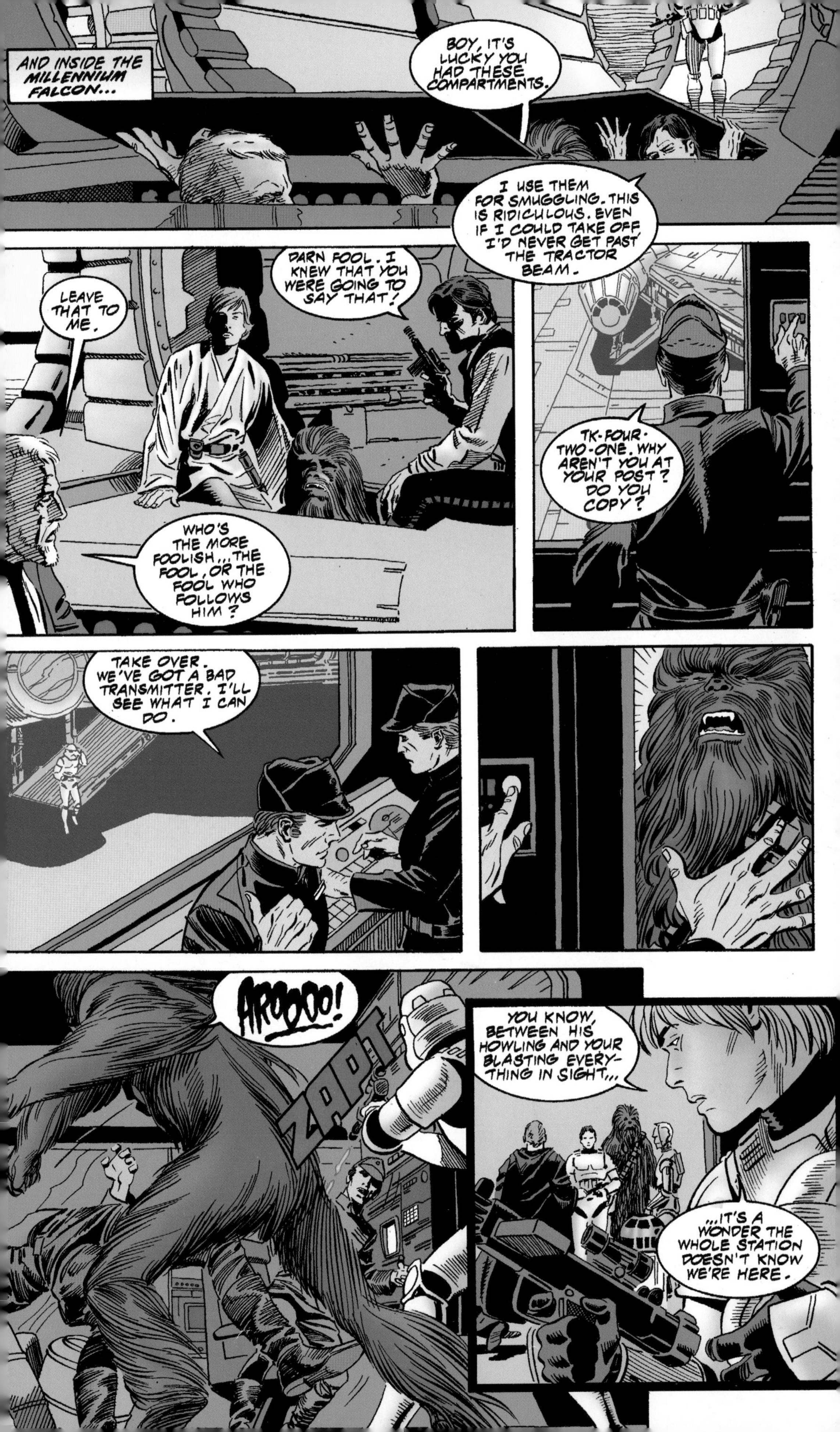
AND INSIDE THE MILLENNIUM FALCON...
BOY, IT'S LUCKY YOU HAD THESE COMPARTMENTS.
I USE THEM FOR SMUGGLING. THIS IS RIDICULOUS. EVEN IF I COULD TAKE OFF I'D NEVER GET PAST THE TRACTOR BEAM.
LEAVE THAT TO ME.
DARN FOOL. I KNEW THAT YOU WERE GOING TO SAY THAT!
WHO'S THE MORE FOOLISH... THE FOOL, OR THE FOOL WHO FOLLOWS HIM?
TK-FOUR-TWO-ONE. WHY AREN'T YOU AT YOUR POST? DO YOU COPY?
TAKE OVER. WE'VE GOT A BAD TRANSMITTER. I'LL SEE WHAT I CAN DO.
AROOOO!
ZAPT
YOU KNOW, BETWEEN HIS HOWLING AND YOUR BLASTING EVERY-THING IN SIGHT...
...IT'S A WONDER THE WHOLE STATION DOESN'T KNOW WE'RE HERE.

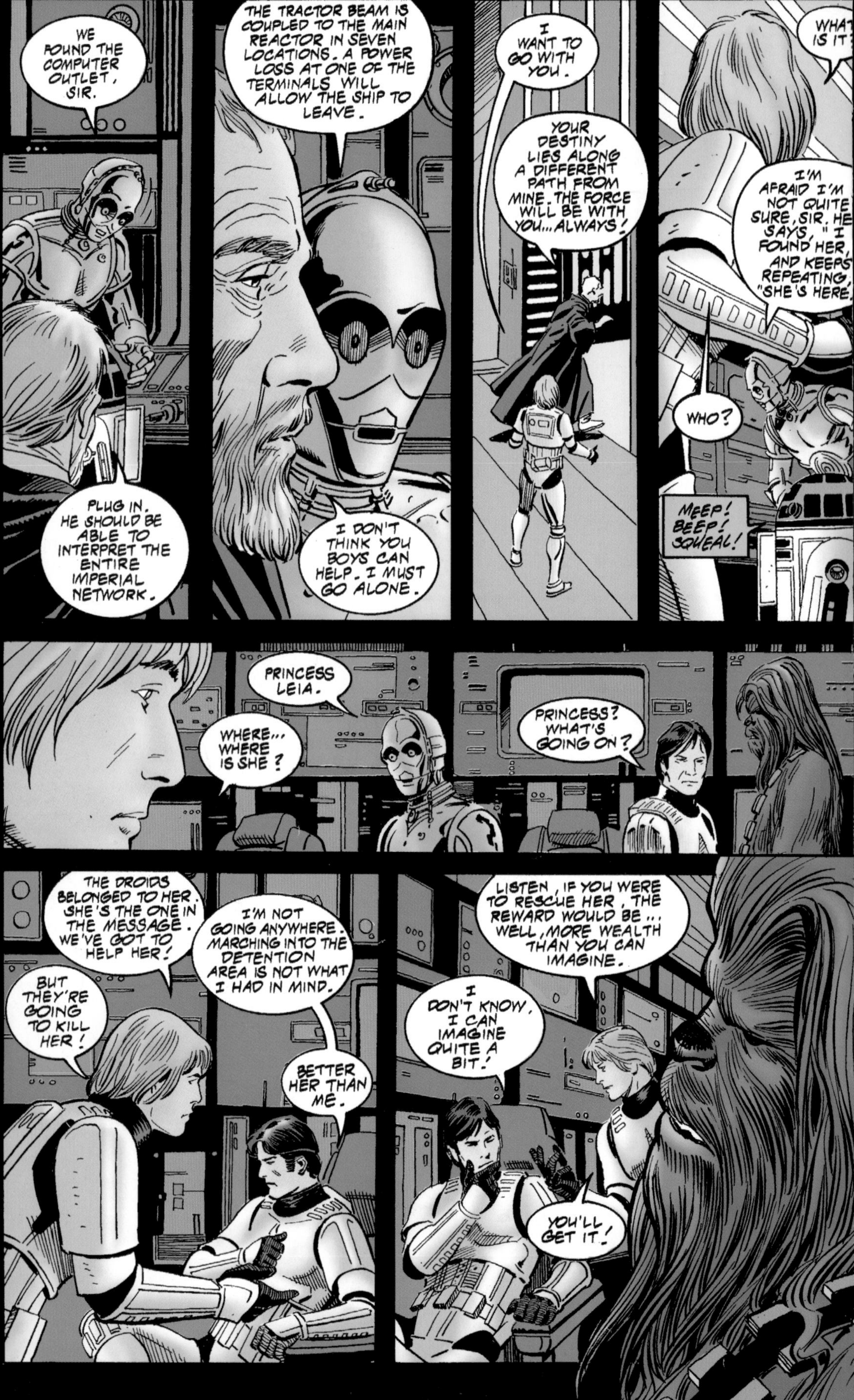
WE FOUND THE COMPUTER OUTLET, SIR.
PLUG IN. HE SHOULD BE ABLE TO INTERPRET THE ENTIRE IMPERIAL NETWORK.
THE TRACTOR BEAM IS COUPLED TO THE MAIN REACTOR IN SEVEN LOCATIONS. A POWER LOSS AT ONE OF THE TERMINALS WILL ALLOW THE SHIP TO LEAVE.
I DON'T THINK YOU BOYS CAN HELP. I MUST GO ALONE.
I WANT TO GO WITH YOU.
YOUR DESTINY LIES ALONG A DIFFERENT PATH FROM MINE. THE FORCE WILL BE WITH YOU... ALWAYS!
WHAT IS IT?
I'M AFRAID I'M NOT QUITE SURE, SIR. HE SAYS, "I FOUND HER," AND KEEPS REPEATING, "SHE'S HERE."
WHO?
MEEP! BEEP! SQUEAL!
WHERE... WHERE IS SHE?
PRINCESS LEIA.
PRINCESS? WHAT'S GOING ON?
THE DROIDS BELONGED TO HER. SHE'S THE ONE IN THE MESSAGE. WE'VE GOT TO HELP HER!
I'M NOT GOING ANYWHERE. MARCHING INTO THE DETENTION AREA IS NOT WHAT I HAD IN MIND.
BUT THEY'RE GOING TO KILL HER!
BETTER HER THAN ME.
LISTEN, IF YOU WERE TO RESCUE HER, THE REWARD WOULD BE... WELL, MORE WEALTH THAN YOU CAN IMAGINE.
I DON'T KNOW, I CAN IMAGINE QUITE A BIT!
YOU'LL GET IT!

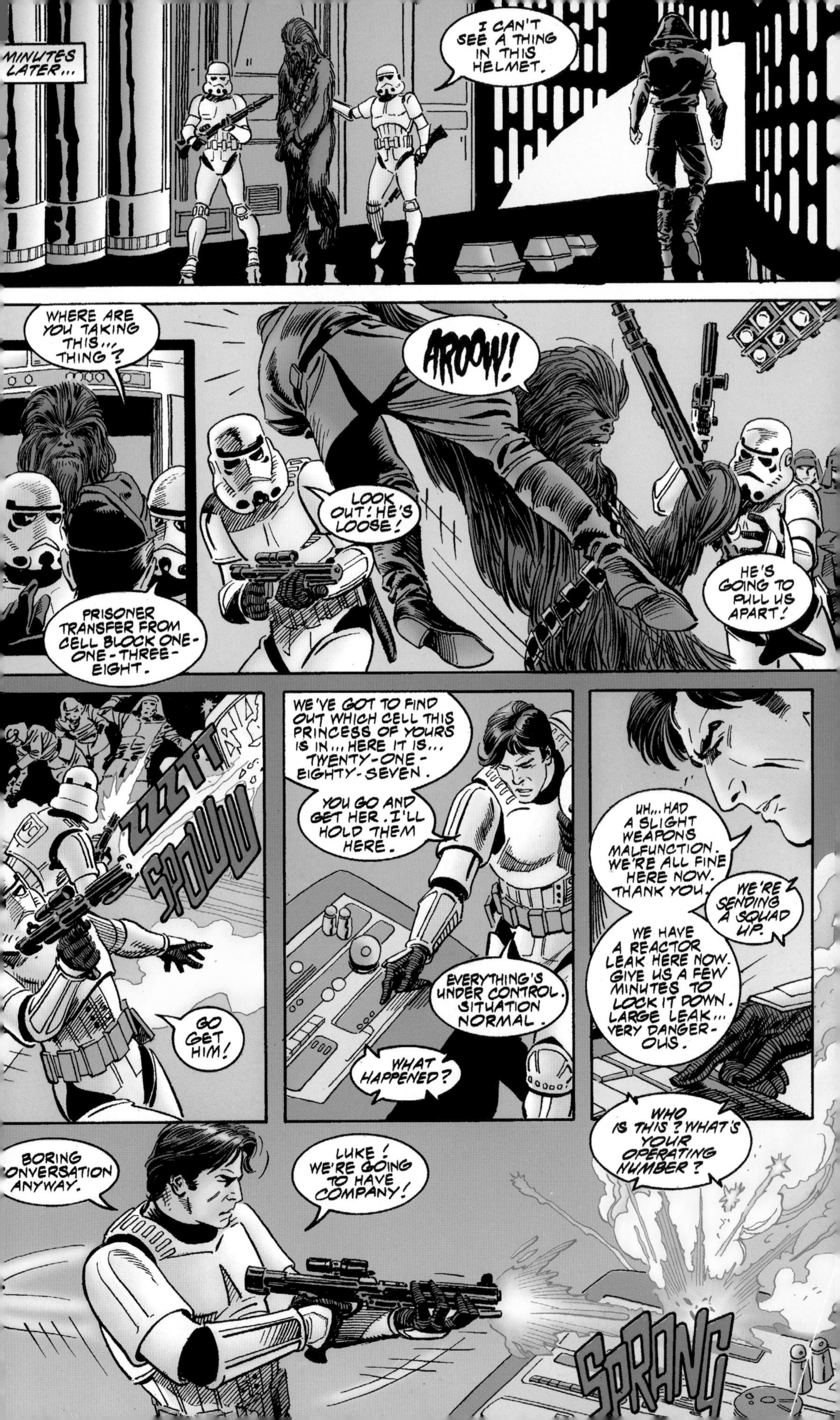

MINUTES LATER...
I CAN'T SEE A THING IN THIS HELMET.
WHERE ARE YOU TAKING THIS... THING?
PRISONER TRANSFER FROM CELL BLOCK ONE-ONE-THREE-EIGHT.
AROOW!
LOOK OUT! HE'S LOOSE!
HE'S GOING TO PULL US APART!
ZZZTT
SPOWW
GO GET HIM!
WE'VE GOT TO FIND OUT WHICH CELL THIS PRINCESS OF YOURS IS IN... HERE IT IS... TWENTY-ONE-EIGHTY-SEVEN.
YOU GO AND GET HER. I'LL HOLD THEM HERE.
EVERYTHING'S UNDER CONTROL. SITUATION NORMAL.
WHAT HAPPENED?
UH... HAD A SLIGHT WEAPONS MALFUNCTION. WE'RE ALL FINE HERE NOW. THANK YOU.
WE'RE SENDING A SQUAD UP.
WE HAVE A REACTOR LEAK HERE NOW. GIVE US A FEW MINUTES TO LOCK IT DOWN. LARGE LEAK... VERY DANGER-OUS.
WHO IS THIS? WHAT'S YOUR OPERATING NUMBER?
BORING CONVERSATION ANYWAY.
LUKE! WE'RE GOING TO HAVE COMPANY!
SPRANG

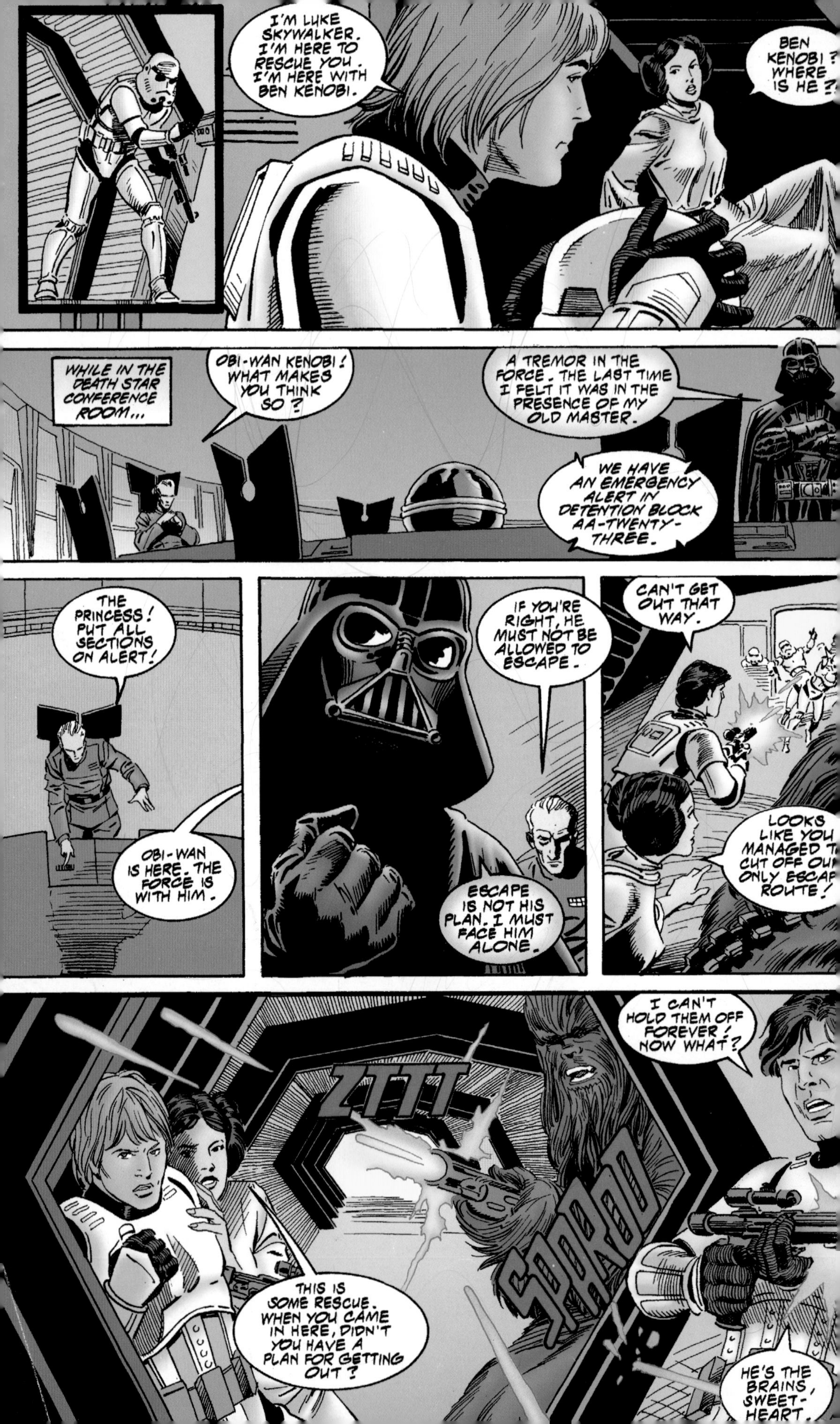
I'M LUKE SKYWALKER. I'M HERE TO RESCUE YOU. I'M HERE WITH BEN KENOBI.
BEN KENOBI? WHERE IS HE?!
WHILE IN THE DEATH STAR CONFERENCE ROOM...
OBI-WAN KENOBI! WHAT MAKES YOU THINK SO?
A TREMOR IN THE FORCE. THE LAST TIME I FELT IT WAS IN THE PRESENCE OF MY OLD MASTER.
WE HAVE AN EMERGENCY ALERT IN DETENTION BLOCK AA-TWENTY-THREE.
THE PRINCESS! PUT ALL SECTIONS ON ALERT!
OBI-WAN IS HERE. THE FORCE IS WITH HIM.
IF YOU'RE RIGHT, HE MUST NOT BE ALLOWED TO ESCAPE.
ESCAPE IS NOT HIS PLAN. I MUST FACE HIM ALONE.
CAN'T GET OUT THAT WAY.
LOOKS LIKE YOU MANAGED T CUT OFF OU ONLY ESCAP ROUTE!
ZTTT
I CAN'T HOLD THEM OFF FOREVER! NOW WHAT?
THIS IS SOME RESCUE. WHEN YOU CAME IN HERE, DIDN'T YOU HAVE A PLAN FOR GETTING OUT?
HE'S THE BRAINS, SWEET-HEART.

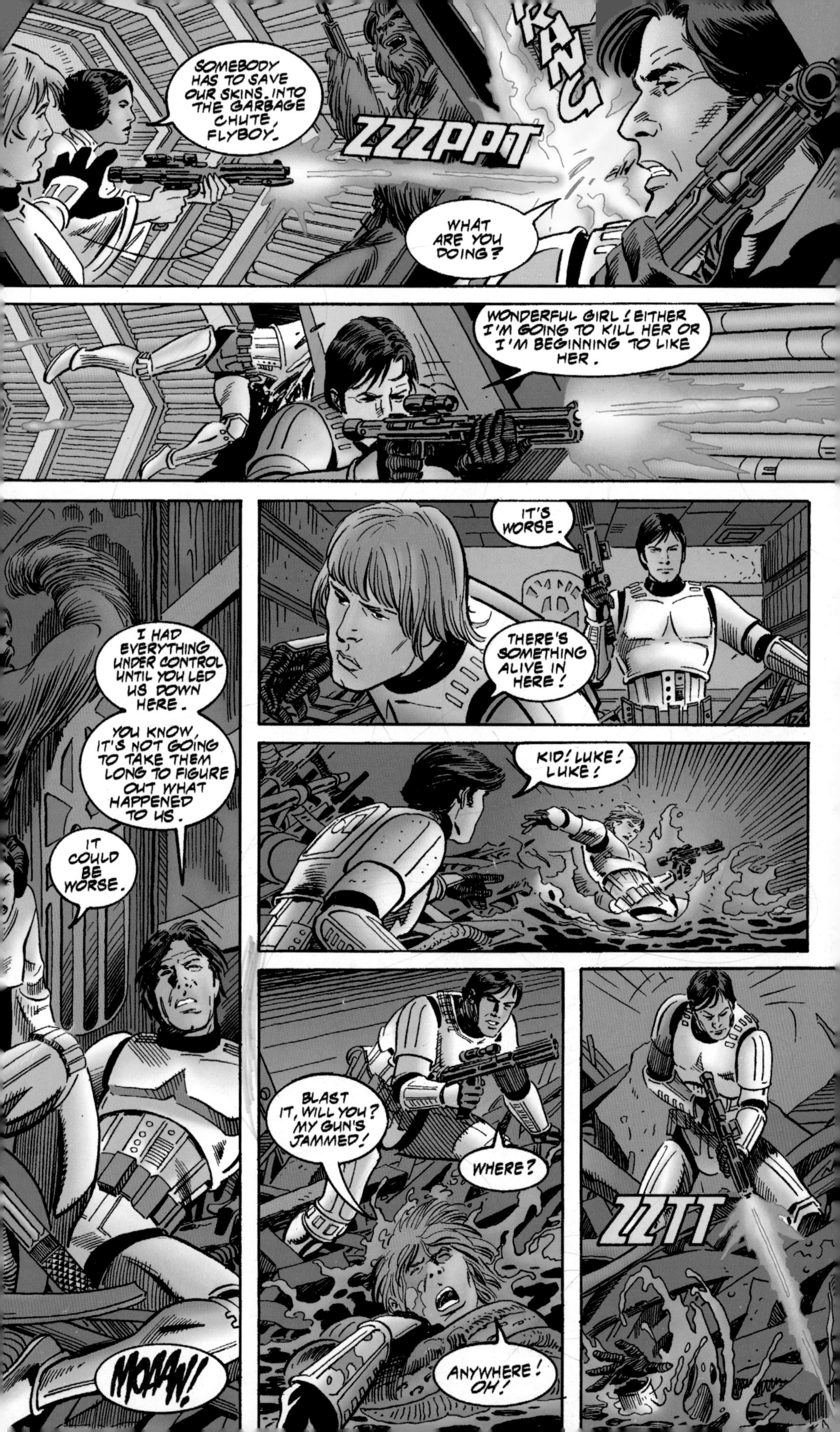
SOMEBODY HAS TO SAVE OUR SKINS. INTO THE GARBAGE CHUTE, FLYBOY.
ZZZPPPT
KRANG
WHAT ARE YOU DOING?
WONDERFUL GIRL! EITHER I'M GOING TO KILL HER OR I'M BEGINNING TO LIKE HER.
I HAD EVERYTHING UNDER CONTROL UNTIL YOU LED US DOWN HERE.
YOU KNOW, IT'S NOT GOING TO TAKE THEM LONG TO FIGURE OUT WHAT HAPPENED TO US.
IT COULD BE WORSE.
MOAAN!
IT'S WORSE.
THERE'S SOMETHING ALIVE IN HERE!
KID! LUKE! LUKE!
BLAST IT, WILL YOU? MY GUN'S JAMMED!
WHERE?
ANYWHERE! OH!
ZZTT

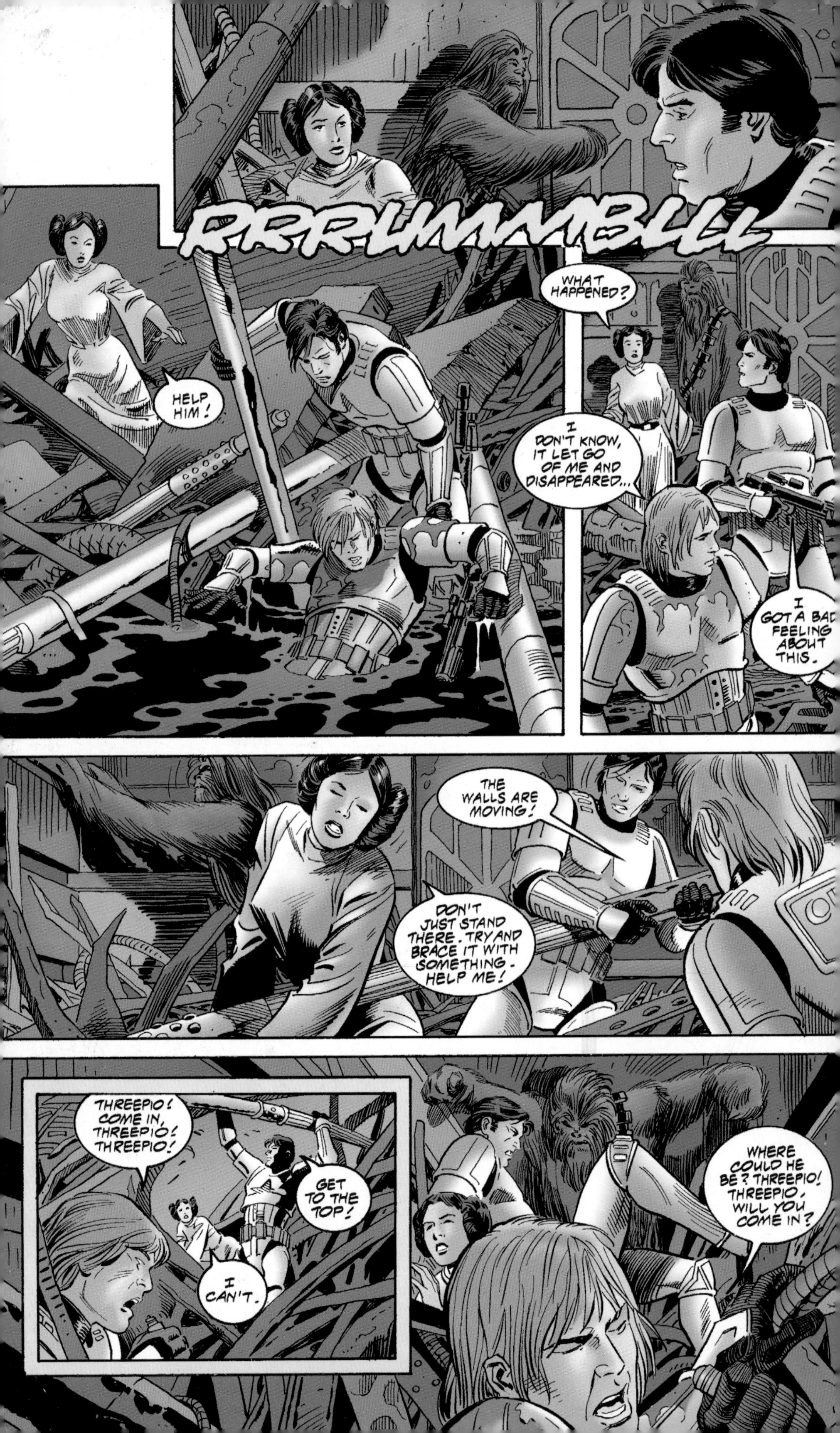
RRRUMMBLL
HELP HIM!
WHAT HAPPENED?
I DON'T KNOW, IT LET GO OF ME AND DISAPPEARED...
I GOT A BAD FEELING ABOUT THIS.
THE WALLS ARE MOVING!
DON'T JUST STAND THERE. TRY AND BRACE IT WITH SOMETHING. HELP ME!
THREEPIO! COME IN, THREEPIO! THREEPIO!
GET TO THE TOP!
I CAN'T.
WHERE COULD HE BE? THREEPIO! THREEPIO, WILL YOU COME IN?

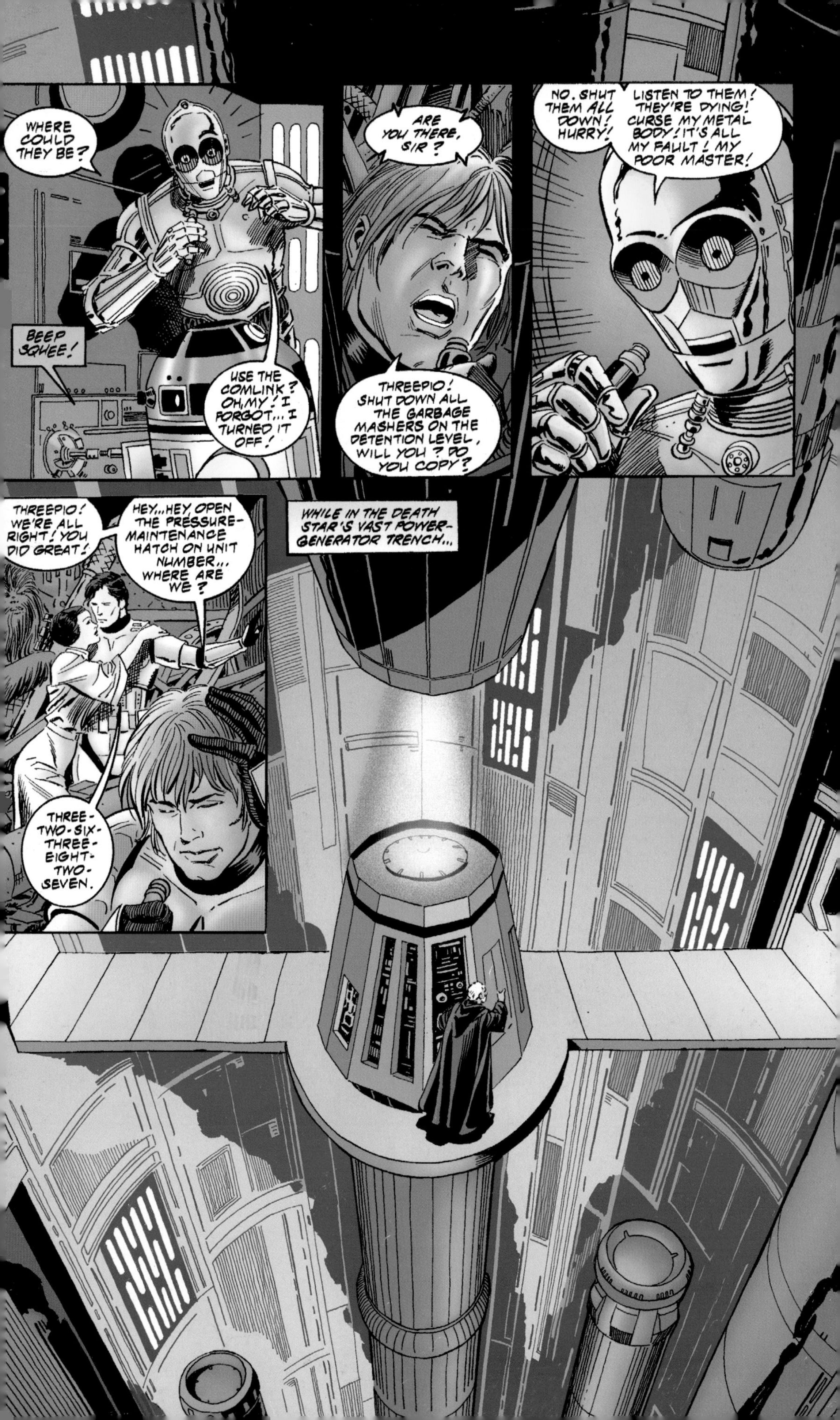
WHERE COULD THEY BE?
BEEP SQUEE!
USE THE COMLINK? OH, MY! I FORGOT... I TURNED IT OFF!
ARE YOU THERE, SIR?
THREEPIO! SHUT DOWN ALL THE GARBAGE MASHERS ON THE DETENTION LEVEL, WILL YOU? DO YOU COPY?
NO. SHUT THEM ALL DOWN! HURRY!
LISTEN TO THEM! THEY'RE DYING! CURSE MY METAL BODY! IT'S ALL MY FAULT! MY POOR MASTER!
THREEPIO! WE'RE ALL RIGHT! YOU DID GREAT!
HEY... HEY, OPEN THE PRESSURE-MAINTENANCE HATCH ON UNIT NUMBER... WHERE ARE WE?
THREE-TWO-SIX-THREE-EIGHT-TWO-SEVEN.
WHILE IN THE DEATH STAR'S VAST POWER-GENERATOR TRENCH...

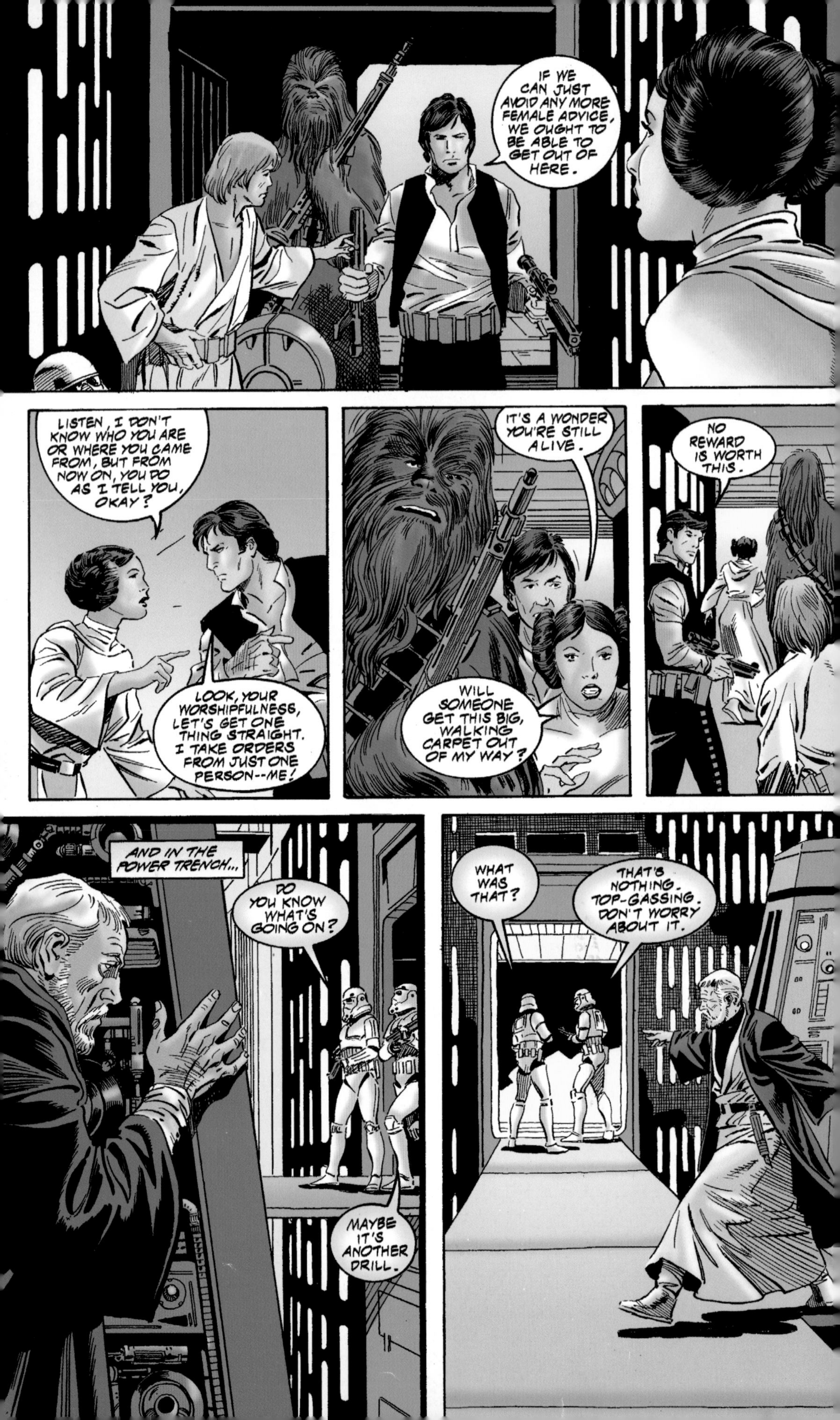
IF WE CAN JUST AVOID ANY MORE FEMALE ADVICE, WE OUGHT TO BE ABLE TO GET OUT OF HERE.
LISTEN, I DON'T KNOW WHO YOU ARE OR WHERE YOU CAME FROM, BUT FROM NOW ON, YOU DO AS I TELL YOU, OKAY?
LOOK, YOUR WORSHIPFULNESS, LET'S GET ONE THING STRAIGHT. I TAKE ORDERS FROM JUST ONE PERSON--ME!
IT'S A WONDER YOU'RE STILL ALIVE.
WILL SOMEONE GET THIS BIG, WALKING CARPET OUT OF MY WAY?
NO REWARD IS WORTH THIS.
AND IN THE POWER TRENCH...
DO YOU KNOW WHAT'S GOING ON?
MAYBE IT'S ANOTHER DRILL.
WHAT WAS THAT?
THAT'S NOTHING. TOP-GASSING. DON'T WORRY ABOUT IT.

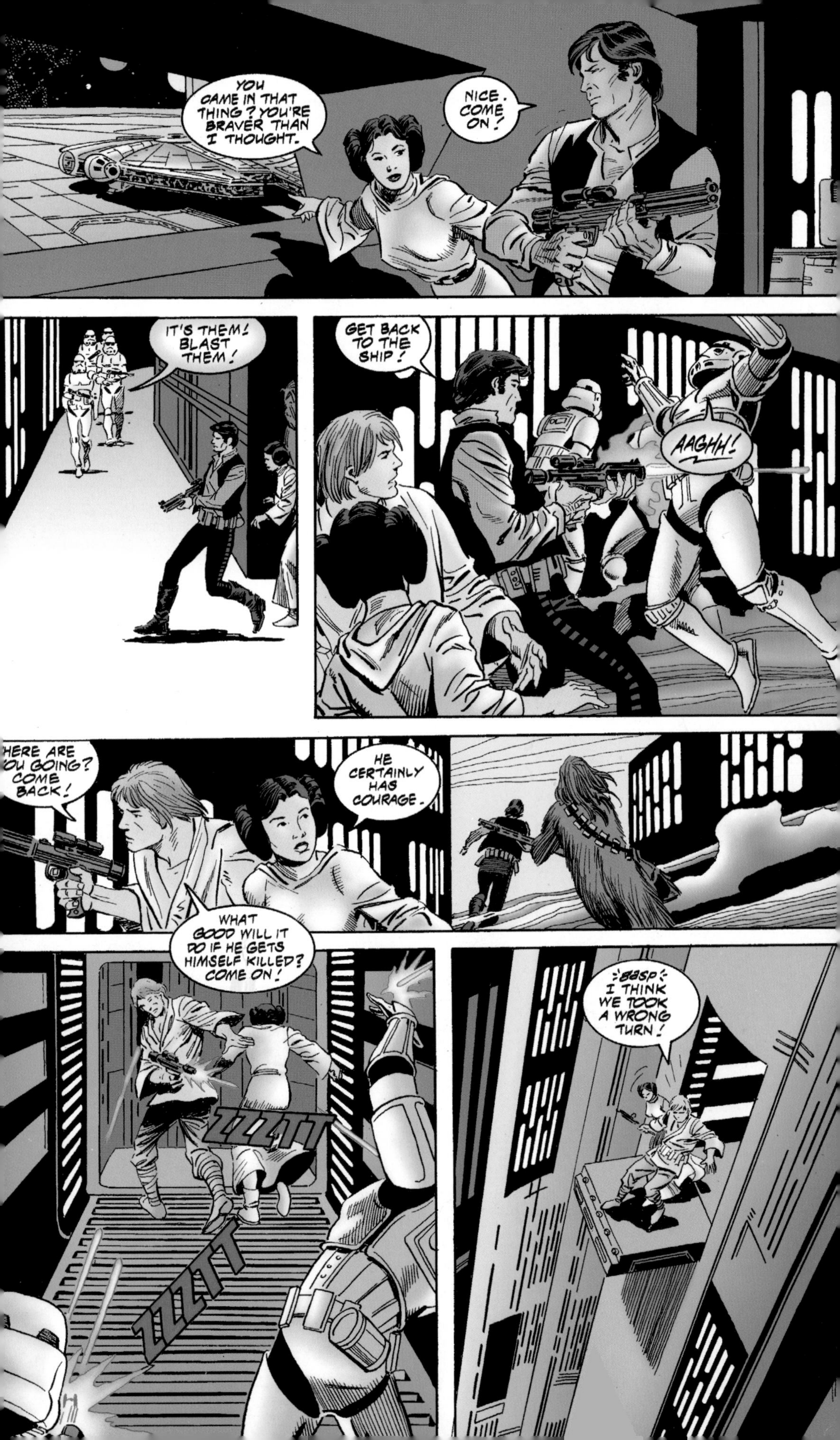
YOU CAME IN THAT THING? YOU'RE BRAVER THAN I THOUGHT.
NICE. COME ON!
IT'S THEM! BLAST THEM!
GET BACK TO THE SHIP!
AAGHH!
HERE ARE OU GOING? COME BACK!
HE CERTAINLY HAS COURAGE.
WHAT GOOD WILL IT DO IF HE GETS HIMSELF KILLED? COME ON!
ZZZTT
ZZZTT
:GASP: I THINK WE TOOK A WRONG TURN!

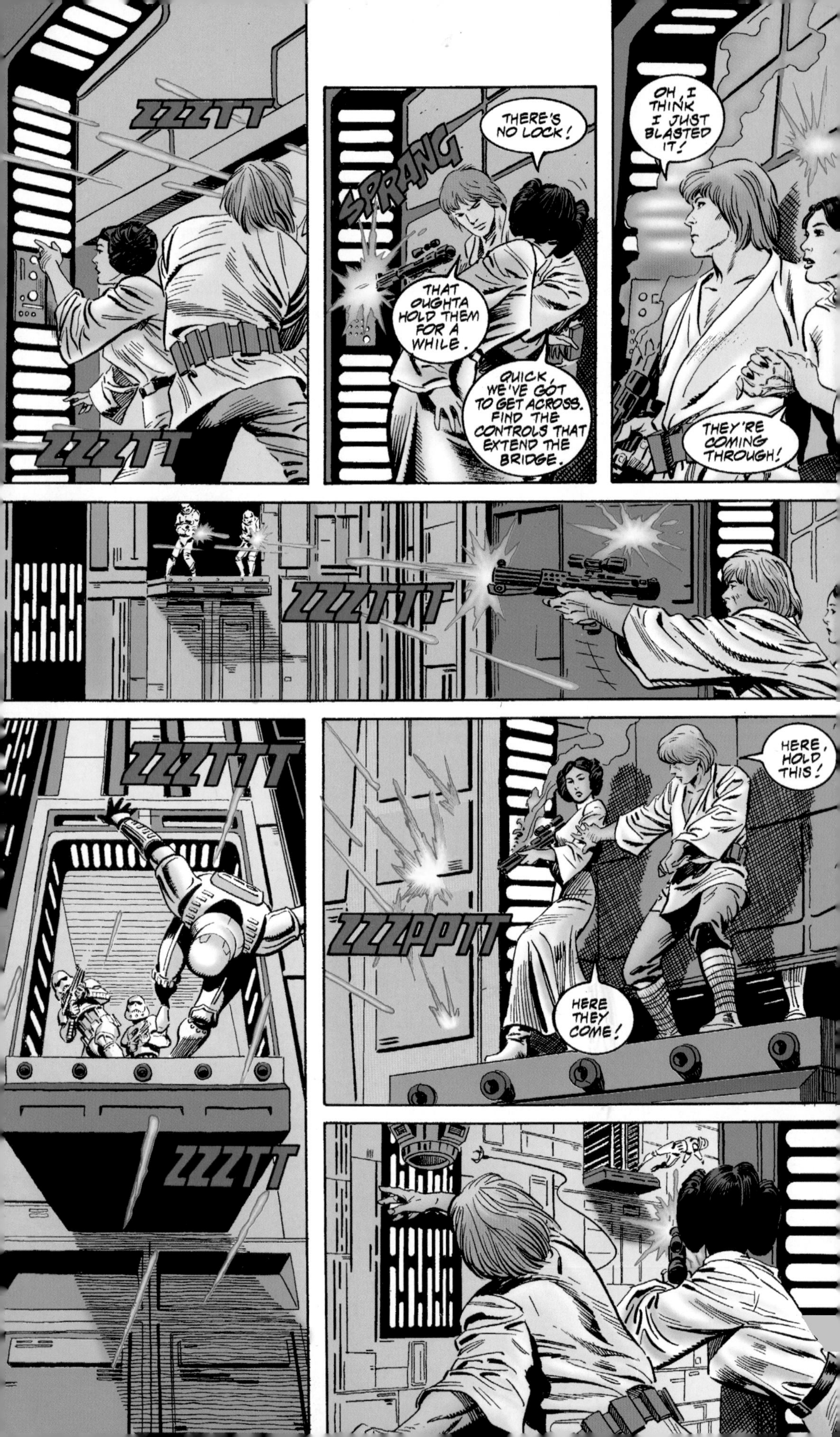

ZZZTT
ZZZTT
SPRANG
THERE'S NO LOCK!
THAT OUGHTA HOLD THEM FOR A WHILE.
QUICK, WE'VE GOT TO GET ACROSS. FIND THE CONTROLS THAT EXTEND THE BRIDGE.
OH, I THINK I JUST BLASTED IT!
THEY'RE COMING THROUGH!
ZZZTTT
ZZZTTT
ZZZTT
ZZZPPTT
HERE, HOLD THIS!
HERE THEY COME!

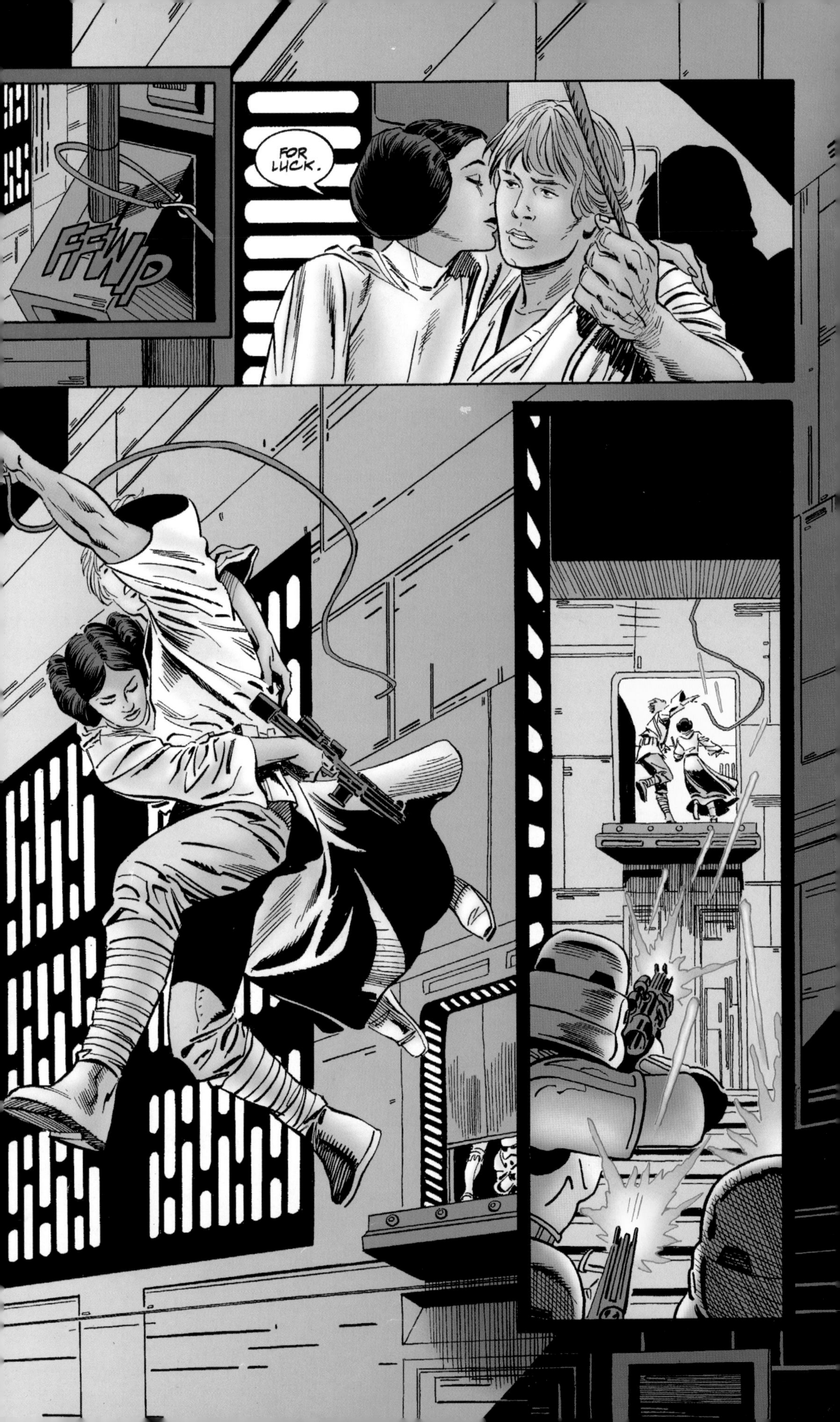

FFWIP
FOR LUCK.

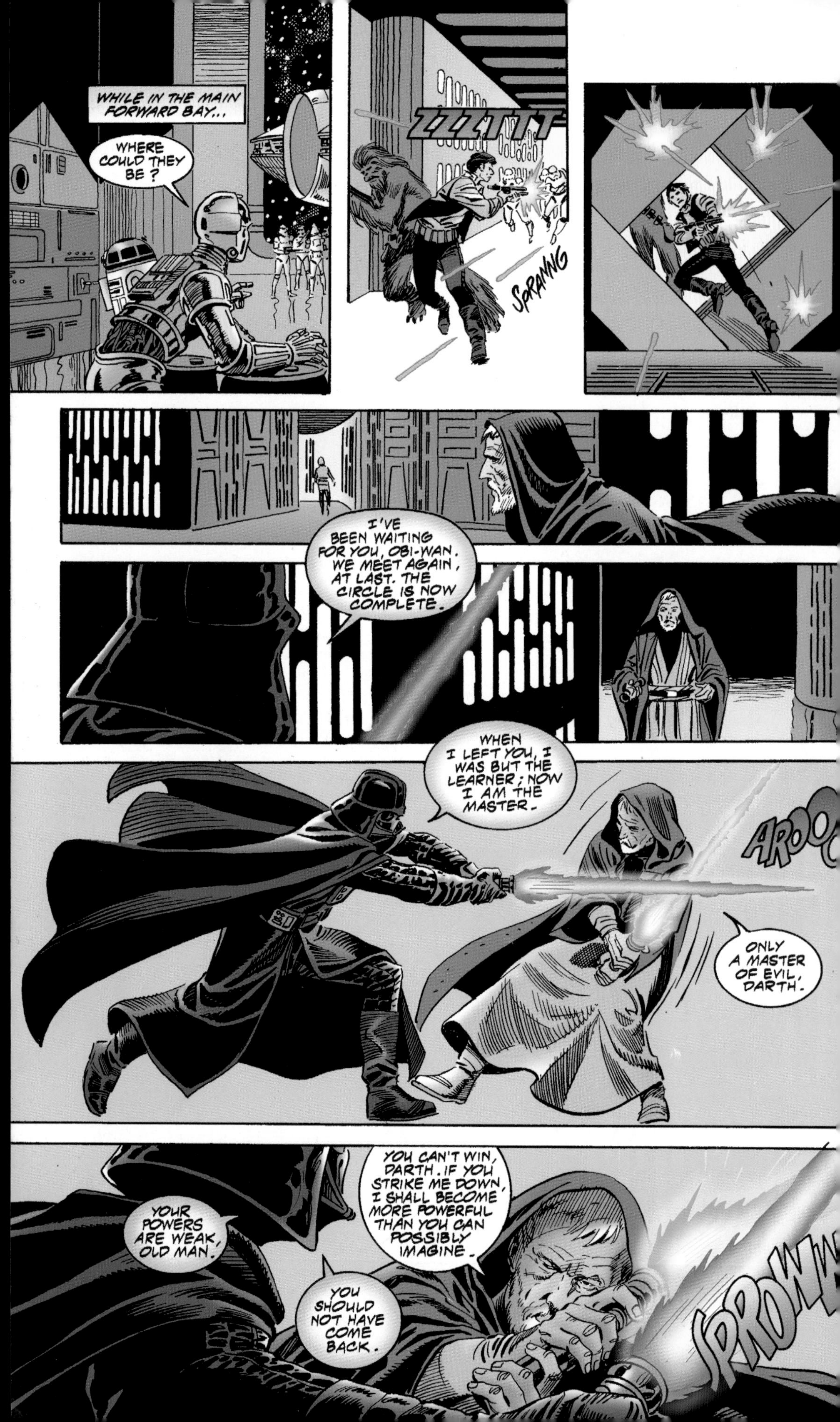
WHILE IN THE MAIN FORWARD BAY...
WHERE COULD THEY BE ?
ZZZTTT
SPRANNG
I'VE BEEN WAITING FOR YOU, OBI-WAN. WE MEET AGAIN, AT LAST. THE CIRCLE IS NOW COMPLETE.
WHEN I LEFT YOU, I WAS BUT THE LEARNER; NOW I AM THE MASTER.
AROOO
ONLY A MASTER OF EVIL, DARTH.
YOUR POWERS ARE WEAK, OLD MAN.
YOU CAN'T WIN, DARTH. IF YOU STRIKE ME DOWN, I SHALL BECOME MORE POWERFUL THAN YOU CAN POSSIBLY IMAGINE.
YOU SHOULD NOT HAVE COME BACK.

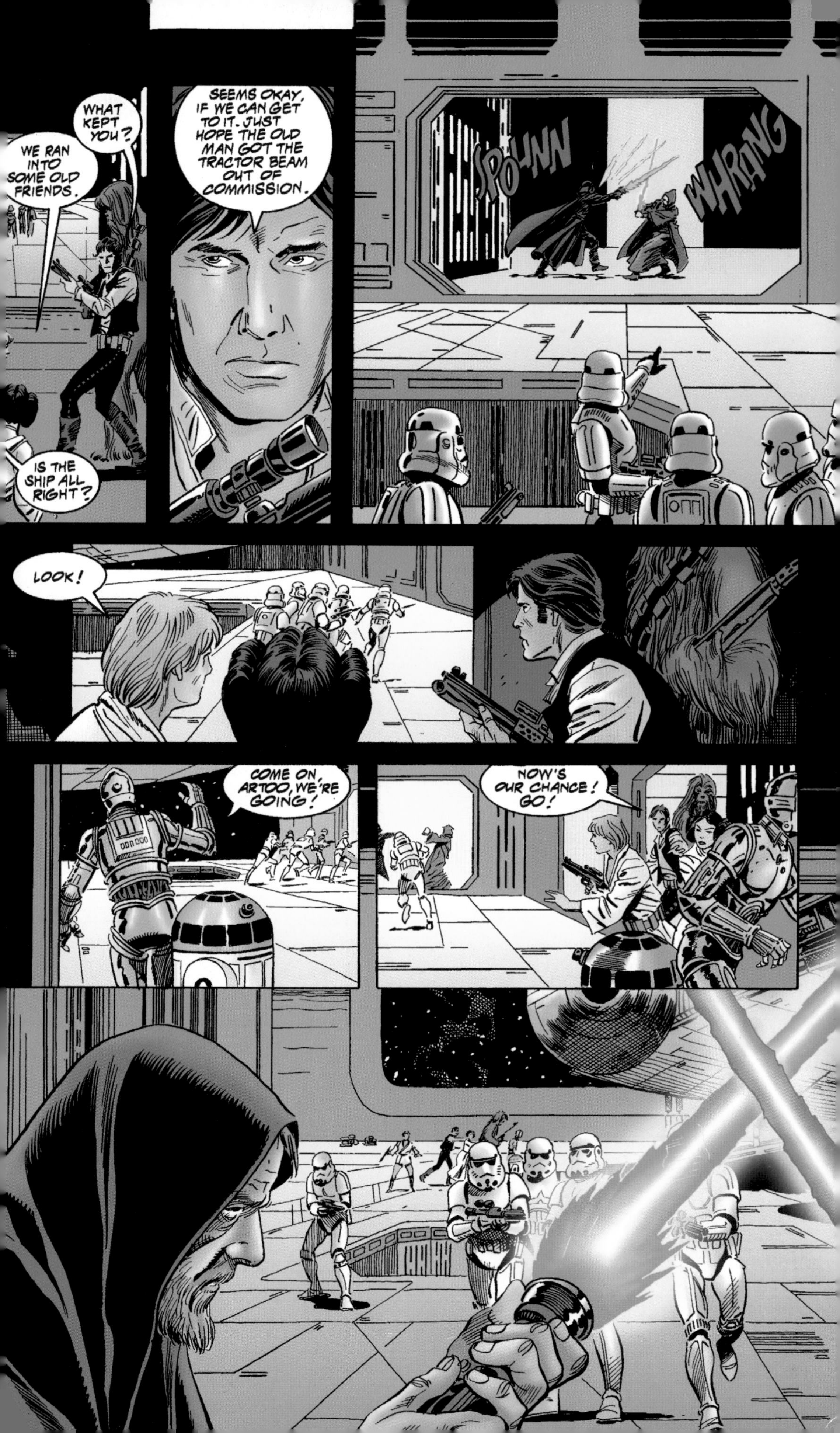
WHAT KEPT YOU?
WE RAN INTO SOME OLD FRIENDS.
IS THE SHIP ALL RIGHT?
SEEMS OKAY, IF WE CAN GET TO IT. JUST HOPE THE OLD MAN GOT THE TRACTOR BEAM OUT OF COMMISSION.
SPOHNN
WHRANG
LOOK!
COME ON, ARTOO, WE'RE GOING!
NOW'S OUR CHANCE! GO!

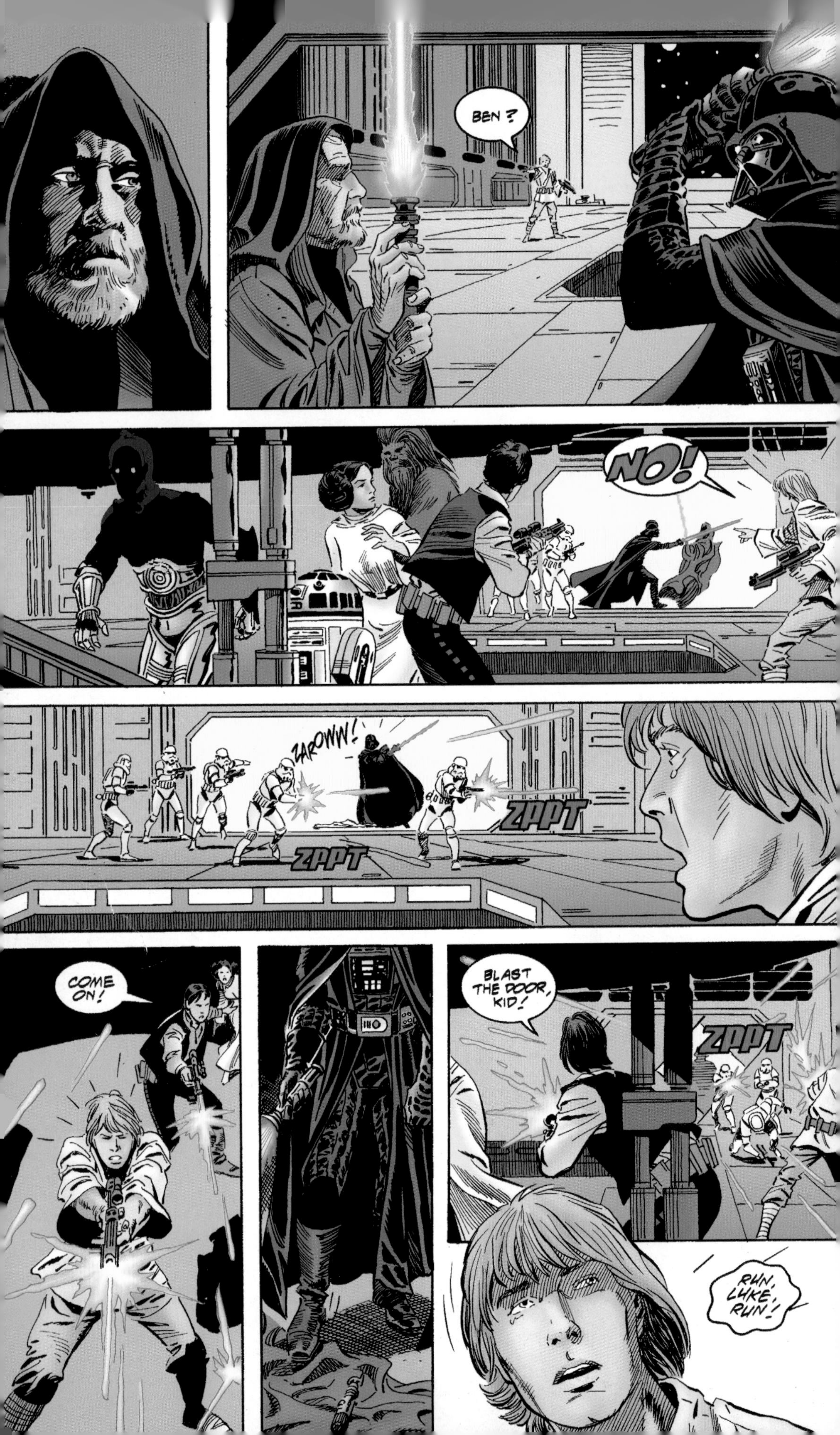
BEN ?
NO!
ZAROWW!
ZPPT
ZPPT
COME ON!
BLAST THE DOOR, KID!
ZPPT
RUN, LUKE, RUN!

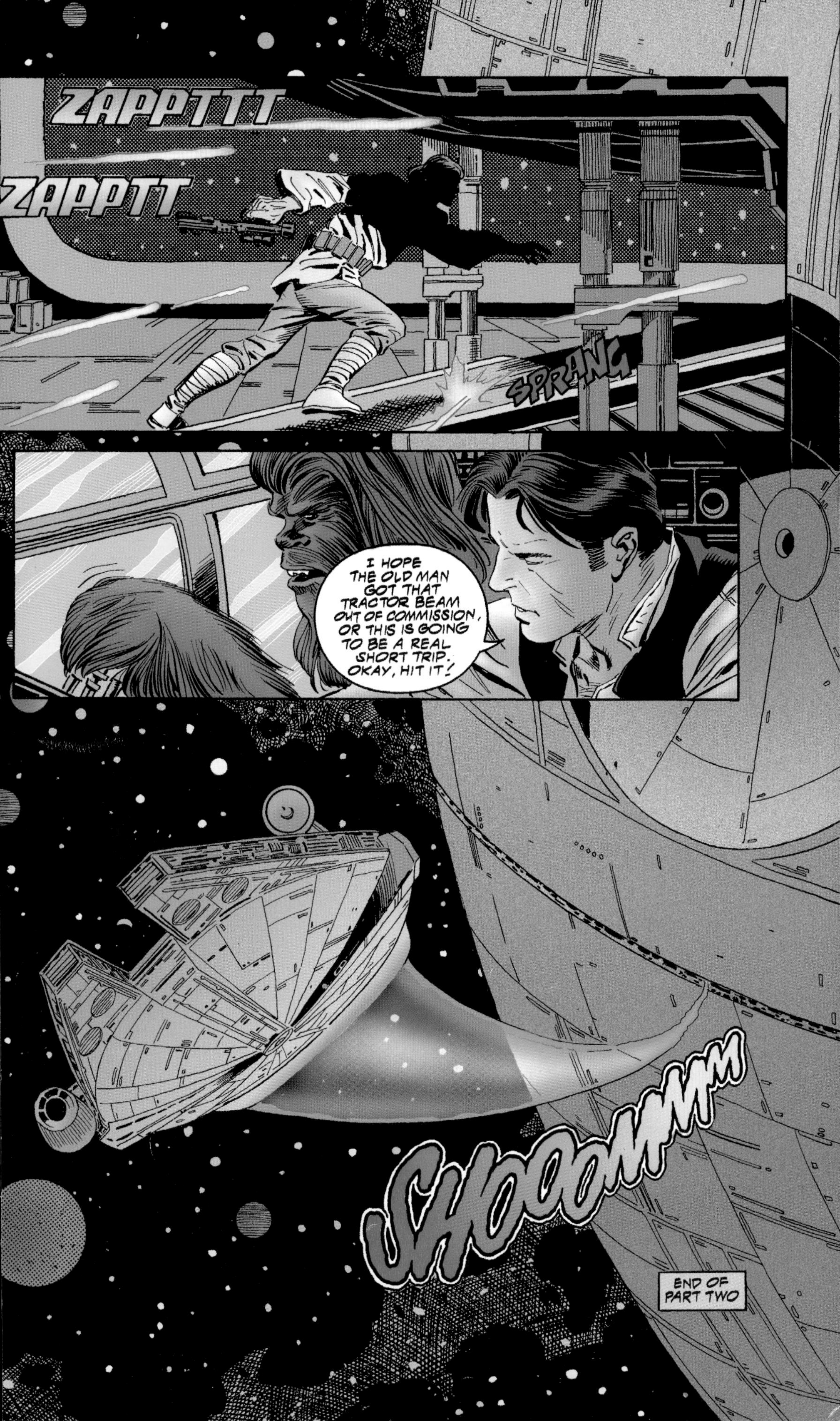
ZAPPTTT
ZAPPTT
SPRANG
I HOPE THE OLD MAN GOT THAT TRACTOR BEAM OUT OF COMMISSION, OR THIS IS GOING TO BE A REAL SHORT TRIP. OKAY, HIT IT!
SHOOOMMM
END OF PART TWO

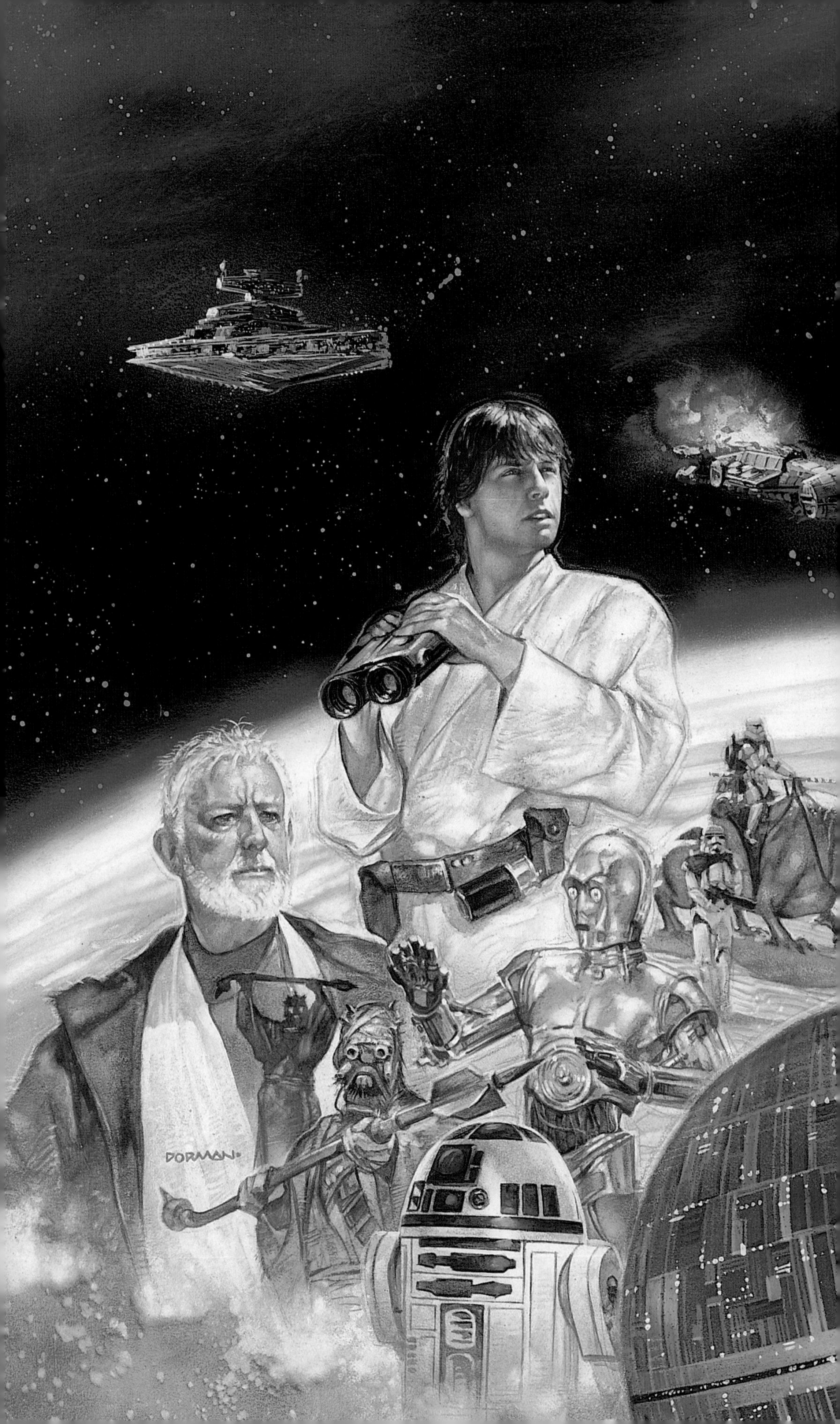
DORMAN

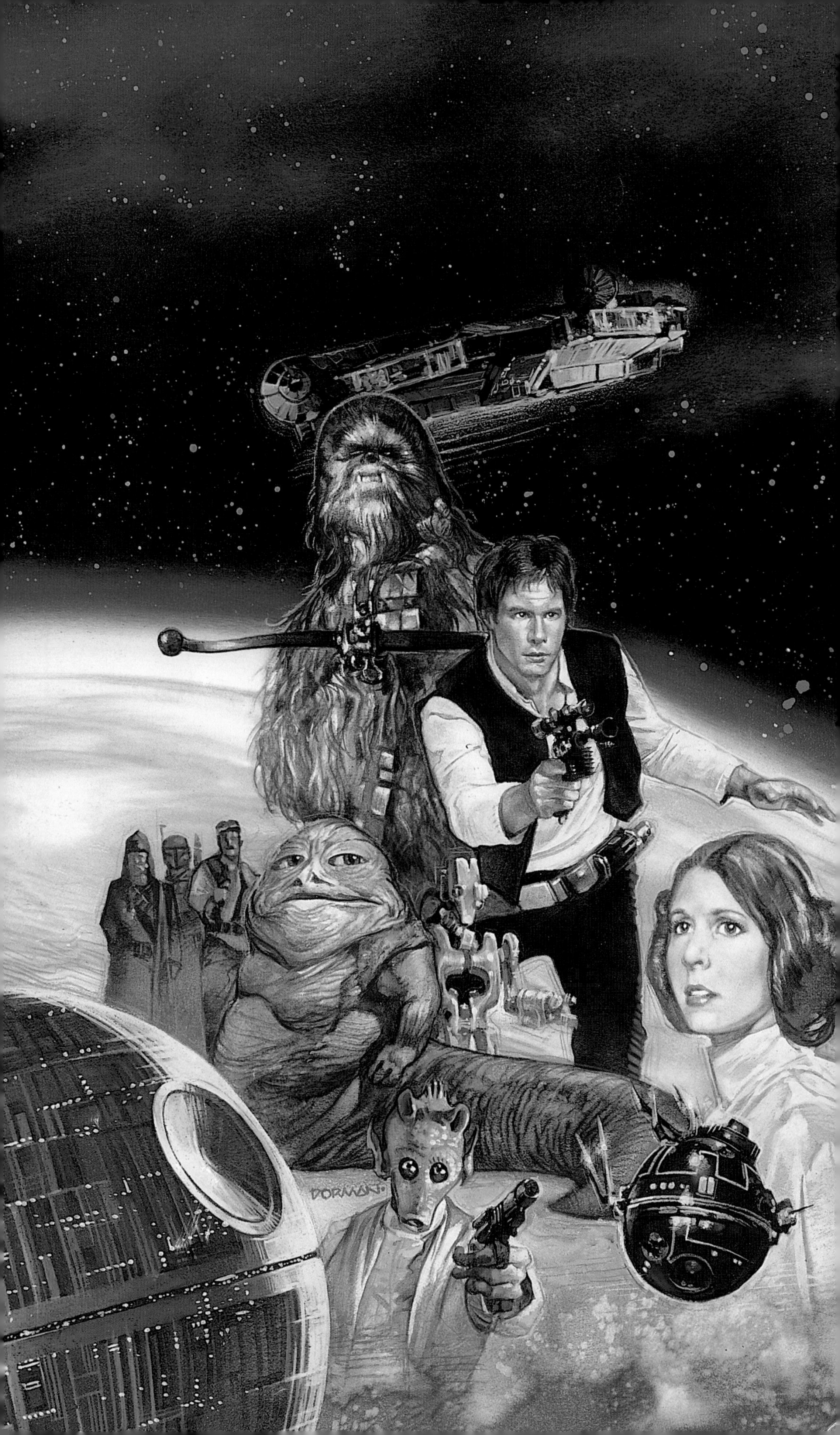
DORMAN

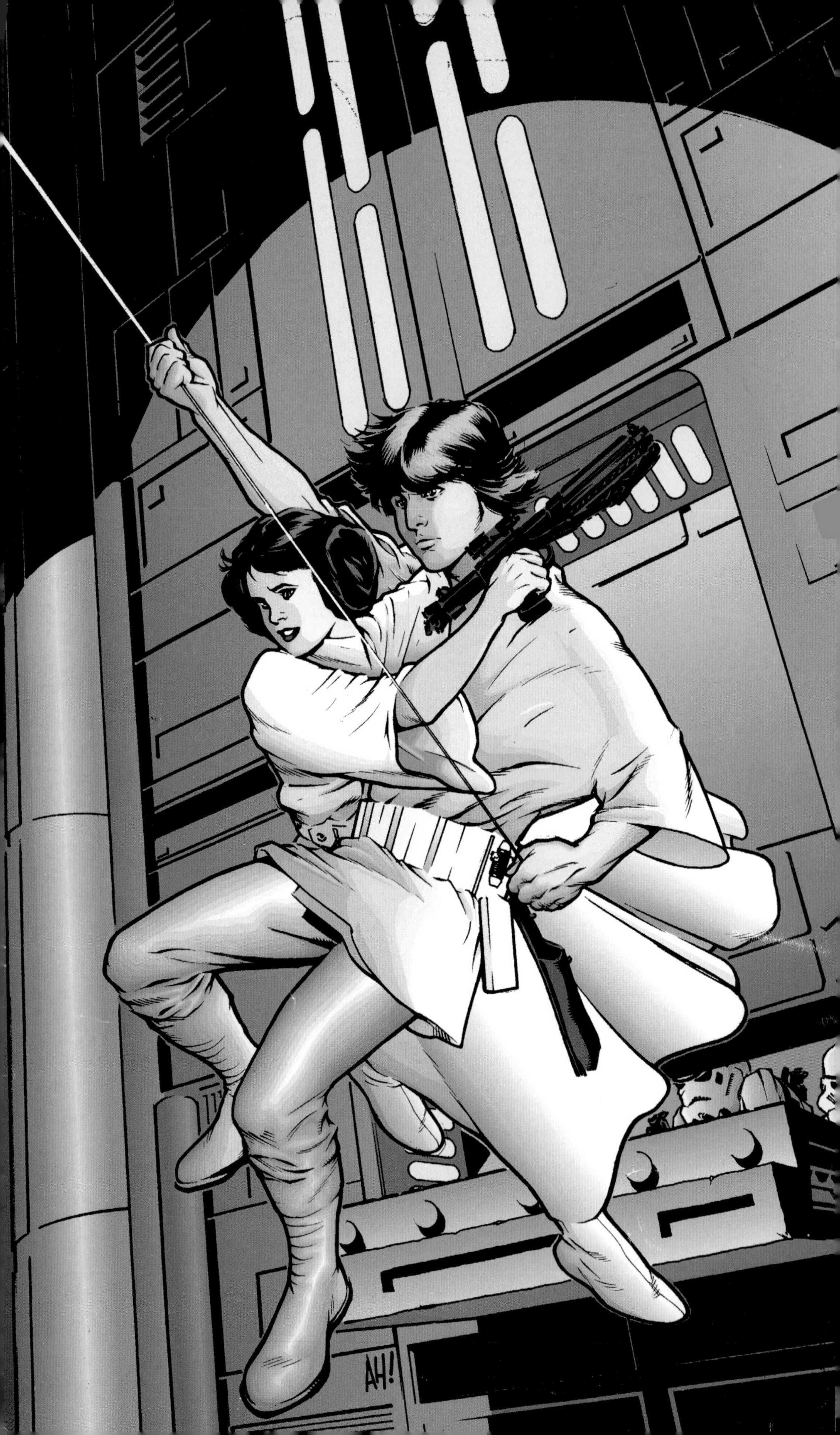